MW01101153

Crooked Lake

Nelson Brunanski

Caronel Publishing
Vancouver Canada

Library and Archives Canada Cataloguing in Publication

Brunanski, Nelson, 1950-
Crooked Lake/ by Nelson Brunanski

ISBN 0-9739121-0-3

(978-0-9739121-0-4)

I. Title

PS8603.R85C76 2006   C813'.6   C2005-905703-3

Caronel Publishing
Vancouver, Canada
www.caronelpublishing.com
www.crookedlake.ca

This book is a work of fiction. Names, characters, and incidents are either
products of the authors imagination or are used fictitiously. Any similarity
to actual events or persons, living or dead is entirely coincidental.

Cover Art: Noel Brunanski
Cover Design: Gerry Mayer

Printed and bound in Canada

for my wife, Carole Clement

Acknowledgements

Craig Brunanski for all his editing help; Paul Grescoe, whose encouragement gave me the nerve to carry on; Noel Brunanski and Gerry Mayer for cover art and design; Stephen Scriver for his advice and oft used quotes; Dean and Cheryl Hildebrandt for providing inspiration; Trent Brunanski, Lynn Wittenberg, Mette Pedersen, Ed Brunanski, Paul Grescoe, Noel Brunanski, Doug Glazer, Stephen Scriver and Leslie Brunanski for reading early drafts of *Crooked Lake*. A special thanks to Trent and Noel Brunanski for their continued support; and to Ed and Jean Brunanski for giving me life and love.

1

I was standing in front of the Lucky Dollar Bakery chewing on a doughnut when I spotted a friend of mine step out of the post office and head across Main Street. He didn't look before crossing the street, and that can be hazardous to your health. But then, the small town of Crooked Lake, Saskatchewan, is a place where you can still get away with it. Usually.

I waved my bakery bags. "Morning, Nick."

Two pick-ups were stopped in the street, diesel engines rattling, their drivers visiting in loud voices. Nick detoured around them with a look that was anything but neighbourly.

"Doughnut?" I offered.

He ignored me and kept walking towards his dusty five-year-old Blazer.

"What's up?" I said.

When he reached his truck he wheeled around, turning his un-neighbourly look on me. "You should know," he said.

"I should know?" I raised my bags in innocence.

"It's no joke," he said, opening the Blazer's door and hoisting himself into his seat. "I just got fuckin' fired." He slammed the door. The truck was cloaked in dust for an instant.

"What the hell are you talking about?" I shouted at the closed window. He paused with his head down, then pulled a crumpled sheet of paper from his shirt pocket and shoved it at me. I waited for the window to come down and took the paper. It read:

To: *Nick Taylor*
From: *The Board of Directors*
          Crooked Lake Regional Park and Golf Course
Re: *Head Greens Keeper Position*
          The Board has voted not to renew your contract as Head
          Greens Keeper. We thank you for past service, and
          request that you remove any personal items you may have
          on park property. Please leave all keys with the gate
          attendant.

"Jesus. What did Les say about this?" I asked, glancing in the direction of the post office.

Nick looked straight ahead, hands on the wheel, saying nothing.

"I'll go talk to him," I said.

"Don't bother, it's like talking to a goddamn two by four." He fired up the Blazer and revved the engine. "It's not him," he said, punching in the clutch, "it's those other sons of bitches, like that fucking Harvey Kristoff." Without another word he released the clutch and peeled out, missing the idling pick-ups by only a few feet. One of the drivers waved a fist.

I walked across the street to see Les Thatcher, the assistant postmaster and park board chairperson. As I entered the post office his attention was on his girlfriend who stood at the counter chatting at him. They'd been dating for so long that people had quit speculating as to when the big day would come; it apparently wouldn't. Still, Les looked a little harried.

While I retrieved mail from my box, I examined the aerial photo of Crooked Lake, circa 1960, that shared the wall with a stamp dispenser and a Canadian flag. The picture, displaying the town sandwiched between highway and railway, had dulled, despite colourful touchups. You could just make out the rows of trees along the broad streets and see the lake, which was within spitting distance and had given the town its name.

Other than the elevators and the two-story hotel, it was the churches that stood out most in the photo. The Ukrainian Orthodox with its shiny spires, St. Mary's Catholic Church, its grounds occupying two square blocks, and the flat-roofed Kingdom Hall next to the highway. These were only three of the seven churches serving the multi-ethnic community of one thousand.

When Les's girlfriend finished with him, I took her place at the counter. "Les, where the hell do you guys get off firing Nick Taylor?" Two seniors standing next to the mailboxes cocked long-lobed ears.

"It's simple, eh."

I waited while Les assembled the simple explanation.

"The board decided," he said, his voice a little shaky, "it ain't happy with him."

"It ain't happy with him?" I said.

Les fiddled with a rubber stamp and repeated, "It ain't happy with him." It's unlikely Les will ever get the top job at the post office, because like Nick said, he just ain't the brightest lamppost on the block.

"Listen Les," I said, "as chair, it's up to you to call a meeting. I'm damn sure we can work things out." The seniors looked over at Les.

"Well," Les said, "I don't know, eh."

"We need somebody running that golf course," I said, "the season's already started."

Les didn't answer, but his pink complexion turned hotter and his short red hair seemed to bristle against the collar of his two-tone green shirt.

"I'm going to talk to the other board members," I said, "so I would suggest you call that meeting. And by the way, Les," and here I brought my six foot one inch frame to full attention and gave him my meaningful look, which, I've been told, can be quite arresting, "I don't appreciate the way you guys ganged up on Nick while I was out of town."

He got the message. At least I thought so, and the two seniors over by the mailboxes seemed to concur.

Most of us small town Saskatchewan folk eat the main meal of the day at noon, dinner we call it. Our youngest is always ravenous at dinnertime and I was surprised he wasn't sitting at the table griping about it when I got home.

"Stu home yet?" I asked my wife.

"He's staying at school today, helping in the computer lab," Rosie said, draining steamy liquid into the sink.

"Mr. Responsible, eh," I said.

Rosie bent over to slide a baking dish out of the oven and I couldn't help but marvel at how even after twenty-two years and two children, the sight caused a stir in me. Her long blond hair, tied hastily in a ribbon, reached half way down her back. Her fine features and great figure haven't changed much since she was in high school.

She turned from the oven and when she realized I'd been watching her, she flushed a little. "What are you looking at?"

"Nothing," I said. I carried the bakery bags over to the counter.

"Any news?" She nodded towards the mail I'd set down on the hall table.

I shook my head.

She looked disappointed. "Did you at least get the stuff I asked for?"

I winced.

"You didn't forget your doughnuts though, I see." Rosie began chopping celery with some ferocity. She'd recently hinted that my doughnuts were turning into spare tires, but I thought my manly moustache and wavy hair more than made up for it.

"Sorry," I said, "I ran into Nick."

Her look said she'd heard it all before.

"He got fired today," I said in my defense.

"Who fired him?"

"The park board."

"What are you saying, that you fired him? You're on the park board too."

I worked the change in my pocket. "I missed the damn meeting."

"You were up at the lodge, right?" she said, shutting the oven door with a bang. "What's the point of working so hard up there? You do realize this is our last year in business." She enunciated this slowly as though I were deaf or thick in the head.

"You don't really believe that," I said. Rosie is usually the optimist in our family, able to buoy us up when times get tough. And this was one of those times. The fly-in-fishing lodge we'd operated for nearly fifteen years was on the brink of closing because the government had refused to renew our lease. "Things will work out," I said, trying to sound confident.

"How can you say that? We haven't heard a word in weeks." She slumped a little and wiped her damp hands on a tea towel.

"You know how the government works. Don't worry..."

Her deep blue eyes shot me a cold look, as if to say it was all my fault.

Those frigid northern winters can really play havoc with buildings, boats and motors and I had made an early trip to the lodge to make repairs and get things ready. "We have to prepare for the season, don't we?" I said.

"Of course," Rosie said through clenched teeth. She straightened her shoulders, took a deep breath and exhaled slowly. "So, why did they fire Nick?"

"The memo didn't say, but I know damn well who's behind it."

"Who?"

"Harvey Kristoff."

"You really think Harvey got him fired?"

"Who else?" I said. "He's tried before. I guess this time he and Lloyd Hughes corralled enough votes to get the job done."

"I'll call Wilma after dinner," Rosie said, carrying the fresh Jackfish I'd caught up north to the dinner table. "She's probably in a state. Well, sit down, everything's ready."

The fish rested on a bed of Saskatchewan wild rice and was accompanied by a big spinach salad, a real favourite on the lodge's menu. Rosie has been cooking at Stuart Lake Lodge since we opened. During that time her reputation has grown to mythic proportions and it's a standing joke that our customers come back as much for her food as for the fishing.

After clearing up the dishes, I retreated to the loft for my post dinner nap. Besides my comfortable old sofa, the loft houses the family computer. Now call me a Luddite, but I don't like it. And do you know why I don't like it? Because the damn thing sucks up time like a Hoover sucks up dirt. Our twelve-year-old is a testament to that. Stuart can spend five hours straight on a Saturday playing games on the thing. His favourite is something called *Hard Times*, a 3-D murder fest as far as I can tell. Anyway, you can have all that modern gadgetry. I've got enough to keep me busy, and a little quiet time is just what the doctor ordered.

Around two o'clock I awoke to the sound of the food processor whirring, the irresistible scent of lemon rising to the loft. I picked up the phone and dialed Doctor Ray Chow, a fellow park board member, golf partner and friend. He was at the clinic and I caught him between patients. "Hey Doc, how're you doing?"

"I'm good, Bart."

"I was wondering what you thought about this Nick Taylor business? Maybe we could get together and talk?"

"There isn't much to say," he said.

"I'm surprised, Doc. I thought you'd see the lunacy of this, especially at this time of the year. I mean, we need a greens keeper and…"

"We've got one," Doc said.

"What do you mean?"

"We hired an interim guy. It all happened at the last meeting." That's why Les was so closed mouth about it when I spoke to him.

"Where'd you find this guy?"

"As you well know, we are obliged to advertise every spring, and we had to make a decision on the applications that came in."

"When I wasn't there," I said, "that's when you had to make a decision?"

"It was on the agenda, and we had to vote on it. Besides, why weren't you there?" Doc said.

"I was up north taking care of business." Though I could have rearranged things had I *read* the agenda.

"Well, there's nothing that can be done now."

"We'll see about that," I said. "How many applications were there?"

"Well, besides Nick and Andy Meyer," he said reluctantly, "there was one, with some experience."

"Oh. I'm sure he's the best man for the job."

"Maybe not the best. But he's on probation to start with, and besides, as much as I like Nick, you know the board had some serious concerns about him."

"You mean Harvey had concerns." I didn't wait for him to respond. "Tell me this," I said, "did we give Nick notice that he was being fired?"

"I assume things were done properly," Doc said, uncertainly.

"Nick looked pretty shaken up when I saw him with that pink slip in his hand," I said. "I'm sure it was the first he'd heard about it."

"Sorry Bart, I don't have a lot of time…"

"And there's no explanation for why he was fired," I said. "And just a memo, to a guy that's run that golf course for seven years. That's not how we do things around here, and you know it."

"Sorry Bart," Doc sounded distracted, "I've got a patient waiting."

"This thing isn't over, Doc, not by a long shot."

Doc is a nice guy and a hell of a golfer. He moved to Crooked Lake about ten years before, and though he and his wife were only the second Asian family in town—the other one, the Lees, run the convenience store on Main Street—they fit in well and were accepted by the community, maybe even quicker than other new arrivals. Ray has been on the park board for a number of years now.

I heard Rosie talking on our business line to Nick's wife, Wilma. "How can they do that?" Rosie eyed me as I descended the stairs from the loft. "I know he'll do everything he can. Yes, I think the public should know about it too." She listened for a moment. "Well," she said doubtfully, "I'll ask him."

"What'll you ask him?" I said after she'd hung up.

"Wilma thinks someone, meaning you, should write a letter to the editor." She watched me screw up my face and look pained. I hate to get involved in politics. I've got strong opinions, but it's been my experience that expressing them publicly generally does more harm than good.

"The Taylors don't plan to take this lying down," Rosie said, spreading meringue over her lemon pie. "Wilma's already called a lawyer to find out if there's anything they can do."

"Good."

"What did Dr. Chow have to say?"

"Doc is toeing the party line. Damn, I wish I hadn't missed that meeting."

I put on overalls and my sturdy work boots and headed out to the garden to prepare for our Victoria Day planting. By then the likelihood of freezing had usually passed, but of course there were no guarantees. Hell, we'd had frost in July. I checked each of the raised beds, hoeing down any early chickweed before it could take hold, then began turning over the soil, awakening the rich organic earth from its frosty hibernation. These six by ten foot garden beds produce bushels of carrots and potatoes and keep us in salad greens all summer long. As I forked the beds back to life, I thought about Nick.

He really didn't deserve the crap the board was throwing at him. He had changed what was nothing more than a glorified cow pasture into a well-respected nine-hole golf course. He'd rebuilt most of the greens, he'd even put up an impressive pro-shop. But still, there were those that wanted him out.

Granted there had been a few setbacks recently, but these had been small ones, with the exception of the fifteen hundred dollars that went missing at the tournament last fall. The townspeople were not amused when the story appeared in the *Saskatoon Star Phoenix* under the heading, *Is Crooked Lake Crooked?* People speculated as to what might have happened to the cash. Some thought maybe kids got at it, but Harvey made it perfectly clear that he thought Nick had stolen it. The police were called in, but nothing ever came of it, and the disappearance of the prize money remained a mystery.

That evening I was finishing up the last of the work in my garden beds when Rosie called from the house, "Bart, phone." I shoved my fork into the soft soil and went inside, removing my boots so as not to track any dirt into Rosie's spotless kitchen.

"Who is it?" I mouthed.

She hunched her shoulders.

I took the phone. "Hello, this is Bart."

"Bart, this is Corporal Snell."

"Hey Fred, how're you?" Fred Snell came out for old-timers' hockey.

"Fine. I need you to come down to the detachment, Bart."

"Uh, yeah, sure. Can you tell me what it's about?"

"I'd rather not over the phone, if you could come down…"

"It's not about Annie is it?" I said.

"No," Fred said, "it has nothing to do with your daughter."

I started breathing again. "Okay, I'll be right there."

Rosie watched me closely as I hung up the phone. "What's going on?" she asked.

"It was Fred Snell, he wants me to come to the police station."

As I shrugged off my overalls, concern spread over Rosie's face.

2

It was clearly not a routine shift at the local RCMP detachment. Nettie Ostrowski, the secretary, was still sitting behind her desk, though it was hours past quitting time. She was being pestered by a young cop trying to hurry her up on the computer. The desk next to hers was occupied by two more constables engrossed in telephone calls and file folders.

In the largest of three offices, I saw Fred and a couple of men dressed in plain clothes facing an uncomfortable looking Les Thatcher. I was ushered into one of the smaller offices and instructed to wait.

After a half hour of cooling my heels, one of the plain clothes officers came in and said, "John Bartowski?" He was tall, had a crew cut and a round baby face. He wore a long sleeved shirt with navy trousers and black, highly polished shoes.

"Yeah, that's me." I smiled. "But I've been called Bart ever since I was six."

"Please follow me, Mr. Bartowski," he said, straight faced. I followed him into Fred's office.

"Have a seat," Fred Snell said, pointing to the chair that Les had just vacated. This is Corporal Klassen," he indicated straight face, "and this is Sergeant Hutt."

I sat in the wooden chair and tried to make myself comfortable. Hutt occupied the desk and Klassen stood.

Klassen spoke first. "Can you tell us where you were today between the hours of four and six p.m.?"

"Can you tell me what this is all about?" I said.

"We're asking the questions." Klassen fixed me with a straight-faced glare.

"What's the difference where I was?"

"Please just answer the questions," the other detective put in mildly. Sergeant Hutt was round and comfortable. It was obvious he'd been in harness a lot longer than Klassen and had nothing to prove. His gray hair was thinning and his casual short-sleeved shirt was a little wrinkled; a pack of Du Mauriers stuck out of his breast pocket.

I looked at Fred and said, "I was at home."

Corporal Klassen flipped open a small black book, "That's…three eighty-five Canuck Crescent?"

"Yeah," I said.

"What were you doing at home?"

"I was working in the garden."

"Who can verify that?" he asked.

"My wife."

Klassen wrote down my responses with an audible scrawl.

Sergeant Hutt looked over at Fred, who, taking the cue, said, "Bart, there's been a serious crime committed." He let that sink in for a moment and then said, "Harvey Kristoff was murdered." They watched my reaction closely.

"Christ. Who the hell would want to murder Harvey?" But even as I said it, a few names came to mind.

"That's what we're here to find out," Sergeant Hutt said, reaching up to his pack of Du Mauriers as though he meant to take one out.

"You don't suspect me, do you?" I felt a cold flush course through me as I waited for his answer.

"If and when we do, you'll be the first to know," Klassen responded.

"Is Nick Taylor a friend of yours?" Sergeant Hutt asked.

"Why are you asking about Nick?" I said.

"Please just answer the questions," Hutt said. "We'll try and answer yours after we're done."

"So, you are a friend of his?" Klassen said.

"Yes, I am."

"Do you know where he was between the hours of four and six this afternoon?"

"No."

"Did you see him today?"

"I talked to him in front of the bakery for a few minutes this morning, but that was it."

"Did he tell you where he was going?"

"No, but I assumed he was going home for dinner, it was almost noon."

"What did you talk about with Taylor?"

"Well," again I looked over at Fred whose face remained impassive, "Nick showed me a memo he'd just received from the park board."

"Indicating that he'd been fired from his job?"

"Yes."

Klassen seemed pleased about this. "What state would you say he was in, upset, angry?"

"No. I'd say he was disappointed." I remembered the forlorn look on Nick's face.

"Did he express anger towards the board?"

"He may have," I said.

"Did he mention Harvey Kristoff?" Klassen asked.

Just then Harvey's wife Ellen was escorted into the building. Like me, she was asked to wait in the adjoining office.

Seeing the murdered man's wife arrive seemed to motivate Hutt. "And what about you?" he asked, "you're on the board, are you not?"

"Yes." They wanted more, so I added, "I try to see that things get done so people can go out and enjoy the golf course, the park and the beach. I guess you could say that Lloyd and Harvey had their own agenda."

"And what agenda would that be?" he asked.

"I don't know, but at meetings he and Lloyd would argue a point until the rest of us were so damn tired, we'd just give up and go home. And Harvey was already lining things up to take over the chair this fall. But mostly he seemed to have it in for Nick. Soon as Harvey was elected to the board two years ago, he started after Nick. He'd take every opportunity to criticize him."

"What were Kristoff's complaints?" Hutt asked.

"Well, for instance, he had a problem with men's night."

"Tell me about it," Hutt said.

"It's a golf tournament where the best scores pick up cash prizes and some goofy presentations are made in the clubhouse. There's a drink cart that runs around the course selling beer and high balls; it's a night for the guys to get together. Harvey didn't like Nick participating in men's night."

"Why not?" Hutt said.

"Exactly," I said. "Most of us thought it was good public relations to have Nick out there mixing with the golfers, and besides, I happen to know he flubbed a few shots from time to time just so he wouldn't win too often. But Harvey was opposed to an employee of the golf course playing for course money and prizes."

Klassen, who had begun pacing said, "What else?"

"There's been the odd foul up in the past couple of years and Harvey made no bones about who he considered at fault."

"What sort of foul ups?" Hutt asked. Fred fiddled with his tie. I hadn't noticed he'd been wearing one until that moment.

"Just normal operating problems that come up in any business. We had to replace the motors in the grass clippers, then there was the frozen water line in the pro-shop. The two new greens might have some drainage problems, but I should point out, Nick wasn't the only one working out there."

Detective Klassen was writing feverishly.

"Yes," Hutt said, "who else is employed there?"

"During the season there are maybe a dozen people. Mostly university students and a few permanent employees like Andy Meyer, he's the assistant greens keeper." Unlike Nick, who was known for his outgoing personality, Andy was a recluse who went about his work showing little interest in anyone or even in the game itself. He certainly never came out for men's night. He applied for Nick's job every year, and every year he was turned down.

Detective Klassen, who seemed to be chomping at the bit to get back into the interrogation said, "What aren't you telling us?"

"What do you mean by that?" I said.

"How come you never mentioned the money that went missing at the golf tournament last year?"

"Never thought of it," I replied. "Am I supposed to remember every detail?" I appealed to Fred.

Klassen rolled his eyes, then said, "Did you know that this morning in front of witnesses, Taylor threatened the board? His exact words—Klassen flipped back a couple of pages in his black notebook—'you assholes won't get away with this'."

"That doesn't sound like a threat to me," I said.

"It doesn't, eh?"

"No. He's been unjustly fired, and he's going to fight it, that's all. Now, how about answering some of my questions?" I said, looking at Sergeant Hutt.

"I'll tell you as much as I can," he said, shifting into a less comfortable position.

"How did Harvey die…I mean, how was he killed?"

"He was hit several times with a blunt metal object," Hutt replied.

"Where did it happen?"

"On the golf course."

"Everybody out there has blunt metal objects," I said, "they're called golf clubs."

Hutt conceded that with a twist of his head. "Look, all I can say is what I've already told you. His body was found next to the green on the seventh hole about five-thirty this afternoon, and he'd been hit repeatedly. That's about it, I'm afraid," Hutt said.

"Do you suspect Nick?" I asked.

Fred was about to say something. Hutt cut him off with a look. "Like I said, our investigation has just begun, and I can't really say any more." Laugh lines showed on his face as he smiled briefly and said, "We appreciate your cooperation, thanks for coming in."

Fred escorted me to the outer office, the officious look on his face now replaced by his everyday expression. "We may have to talk to you again, Bart," he said. "And sorry if they got on you a bit in there."

I ignored that and said, "If those guys think Nick did this, they're crazy, Fred." As I turned to go, I saw Ellen Kristoff being led into the big office. She glanced over to where Fred and I stood. It looked as though she might smile, but the smile turned into a grimace and the grimace led to sobbing. Klassen looked as though he might put a consoling arm around her shoulder, but he didn't.

It wasn't until I got out of the unfamiliar confines of the RCMP detachment that the reality of the thing struck me. Harvey Kristoff murdered. In broad daylight on the seventh hole that I'd played hundreds of times. The seventh is a narrow hundred and fifty yard par three that tempts even novice golfers to try for birdies. It runs parallel to the lake and is considered the prettiest hole on the course. But, too much of a slice and you're laying two off the tee, your ball sinking into the fathomless mud at the bottom of the lake. I drove the eight blocks home through deserted streets. Nearly all the houses were dark at that hour, their occupants safely asleep in their beds.

"So, it's all over town," Rosie said the next morning as she struggled into the house carrying a bag of groceries under each arm. "Helen Mousie was telling everybody who came into the Co-op Store." I took one of the bags from her while she dumped the other on the kitchen counter. "She said the police already have a suspect in custody."

"Who is it?"

"Helen didn't know."

"Nick?" I wondered.

"Yeah, but come on," Rosie said, tucking long tresses of hair behind her ear, "getting fired is no reason to go out and kill a guy." I had to agree with her there.

"Stuart, dinner's ready," Rosie called up to the loft where he was at those damn computer games again. She'd made roast pork for dinner, with a nice corn chowder.

I sat down and started in on my chowder. Rosie had used the last of our frozen corn, adding a pinch of lemon balm that we grow a lot of because it's supposed to keep the mosquitoes away.

"Stuart, get down here please," Rosie yelled, "your dinner's getting cold."

"I don't want any," we heard him say over the sound of gunfire. Rosie frowned at me.

I said, "Stuart, I want to see your butt in this chair, pronto."

Stuart trundled down the stairs. "I'm not hungry."

Rosie touched his forehead. "Are you feeling all right, honey? You don't have a fever, do you? Is everything okay at school?"

"Yeah, it's fine." He dropped into his chair.

"Then what's wrong?"

"I don't know. I just feel weird 'n stuff. You know, about Mr. Kristoff 'n stuff."

Again Rosie and I looked at each other. "Oh Stuart," Rosie said. "Listen honey, your dad was down at the police station and..." A tilt of her head and an arched eyebrow said, *you take over.*

"Yeah," I said, "they have a couple of detectives in already, from the city. They know what they're doing, don't you worry."

"But that's it, I am worried. What if the guy does the same thing to you? I mean, you're on the board 'n stuff too, right. Maybe he's a serial killer and he's gonna kill everybody on the board?"

"Where'd you get an idea like that?" Those damn computer games. "Listen to me." I got down on my haunches in front of his chair, my hockey knee protesting only slightly, and fixing him with my meaningful look, said, "There's no serial killer, and there's nobody going to do anything to me. Stu, those detectives are going to get whoever did this and everything will be back to normal, you'll see." At least that was my hope.

3

With less than three weeks before fishing season opened and despite Rosie's despondency, I kept busy ordering groceries, picking up parts for equipment and calculating load limits on the Twin Otter that would transport our first party to the lodge on June first.

Air charters costing what they do, we have to ensure that we make the most of each flight. In addition to the six fishermen from Denver and their gear, we'll have two or three guides, three outboard motors, hundreds of pounds of food, a few barrels of gas, and of course, Rosie, me and our golden retriever, Butch.

That first week at the lodge can get pretty hairy, like the year we found a mother bear and two cubs living in one of the cabins. They'd broken through a window, and it looked as though the cubs had occupied one of the twin beds while the mother had luxuriated in the other. They had managed to rip the fridge apart, no doubt titillated by some residual scent of food. They even tore a stuffed trout off the wall and devoured part of it before realizing it wasn't the real thing.

By the time I'd finished work around six that evening, rumours were rampant. Nick was the number one suspect in the murder and was being held for questioning.

After a supper of pork sandwiches and pickles, Rosie and I drove over to Nick and Wilma's. There were a few cars on the street and a shiny SUV parked in the driveway behind Wilma's Ford Escort. Wilma's sister Pat answered the door and ushered us into the living room where Wilma sat surrounded by friends and family, including her two kids, Jake, fifteen, and Susan, thirteen. There was also a well-coifed man of about forty, wearing a nice suit, sitting next to her, a briefcase open on the coffee table in front of him. I figured it was his SUV in the drive.

We reassured Wilma and said hello to the kids, then took seats next to other well-wishers. The man in the suit introduced himself as Frank Hendrickson. He practiced law in the city of Prince Albert and had been recommended by Nick's brother-in-law for whom he'd settled a boundary dispute with a neighbouring farmer. While he talked to Wilma, we enjoyed some coffee cake along with cups of strong tea.

On his way out, Hendrickson asked if he could meet with me to talk about Nick's case.

"Why me?" I asked.

He said, "Well, for one thing you're a friend of Nick's and I thought you might want to help."

"Of course I do," I replied.

"And secondly, you're a member of the park board and can probably give me some insight into why Nick was fired." I had already planned a business trip to Prince Albert the following day, so we agreed to meet at his office at two p.m.

The sun shone out of a cloudless blue sky the next morning as I drove into P.A. I had a lot to do before meeting with the lawyer. I picked up the overhauled generator that had burned out last fall, leaving the lodge waterless for several days. Those Texas oilmen were definitely ripe when they left. I stopped at Wadner's to look through a new batch of fly-fishing lures and to grab a couple of new rods. Formerly a fur buying institution, Wadner's had evolved, during the politically correct years, into an outfitters' supply store, changing from fur company to rod and gun shop. But the smell of smoky fur still pervaded the wooden structure and seemed to hang like history on everything that left the store. My stock of lures, leaders and line was low, so I grabbed an assortment, some for deep-water trout and others for casting to big northerns. I also bought shells for my 30-30 bear rifle.

I met Charlie Mackenzie, our head guide, for dinner at the ABC Country Restaurant located next door to the Whoop-up Casino. Charlie had been with us from the start. His family had hunted and trapped at Stuart Lake long before we'd showed up, lease in hand. His knowledge of the lake and sense of humour had pulled us through a lot of tough times over the years.

"So, what's the latest?" Charlie asked, sprinkling salt liberally over his turkey special. "We gonna have a lodge next year?"

"We're doing everything we can," I said.

"I'll bet you are," Charlie said, his weathered face full of fun. He flipped his long braids over his shoulders so they wouldn't interfere with his dinner.

We ate in comfortable silence for a while as we'd done countless times up north.

"You know what the problem is?" I said. "These mining companies have too much influence with the government. They're hand in hand."

"It's the money," Charlie said.

"And the government knows it'll get a hell of a lot more out of Capex International than it will out of me."

The waitress brought our dessert and took away the empty plates.

"We been fishing and hunting at Stuart a long time," Charlie said. "We're not going anywhere." There was finality in his voice.

We finished our apple pie and coffee and said our goodbyes. As I pulled out of the ABC, I looked for Charlie, but he'd already disappeared into the Whoop-up Casino with the five hundred dollars I'd advanced him.

Hendrickson's office was on Central Avenue in an impressive six story, glass building. On the fifth floor I got off the elevator that opened directly onto an oak paneled reception area, and staring me down was one beautiful and bejeweled receptionist. With a pert smile, she asked me to take a seat. Frank Hendrickson appeared a few minutes later, expensive shoes clacking on the ceramic tiled floor.

"How are you, Mr. Bartowski?" he said, offering his hand. "Thanks for coming in." In his office, Hendrickson sat behind a huge desk in a high-backed, leather chair. I sat across from him in a not-so-comfortable armchair. He wore a different suit than he'd been wearing the night before, but just as nice, hound's tooth I guess you'd call it, and a blue tie. I declined his offer of refreshments, and we got to it.

"So," he said, sitting back in his chair and removing a legal note pad from his desk drawer, "as I told you yesterday, I wanted to talk to you, not only because you're on the park board, but because you're Nick's

friend. I should tell you that my function is two-fold."
He removed his rimless glasses. "Initially I was engaged
in the matter of wrongful dismissal, but since Nick is
now a suspect in the murder, I may be called upon to
represent him in the eventuality that he is arrested in
connection with that. If it's all right with you," he
mimed a balancing act, "I will be straddling the two
areas for which I've been retained. I'm interested in the
dynamic between Nick and the board and naturally
between Nick and Harvey Kristoff. "What about Nick
and Harvey? Why the antagonism between the two?"

"Well, Harvey could always find something to carp
about," I said.

"But if Nick was doing a reasonable job at the park,
what was Harvey's problem?" Hendrickson asked.

I leaned forward in my chair. "All this is confidential,
eh? I mean, what I say here is all intended to help
Nick?"

"That's right. Please speak freely."

"I haven't said this to anyone, including my wife," I
said, "but I think Wilma might have something to do
with it."

"Wilma?"

"Back in school Harvey and Nick tangled over her.
First Harvey dated her then Nick skated in and stole her.
I remember the night it happened. We'd just beat the
toughest team in the league and even though Nick had
been harassed by their biggest guys and took a stick in
the face, he'd scored three goals. The crowd loved him.
Nick was talented, you know. In fact, some pro teams
scouted him, but he always came up short. Five foot
eight. Anyway, we were celebrating and I guess being the
hockey hero in a town that was hockey crazy, he looked

pretty good to Wilma that night. She had come to the party with Harvey, who wasn't half bad looking in those days, but left with Nick. See, Harvey didn't play hockey. I don't think he could even skate."

"And *that's* why Wilma dumped him?" Hendrickson said.

"No, but who knows what a kid is thinking. Hell, I don't know what mine are thinking most of the time, in fact I don't think I want to know. The thing is, Nick and Wilma didn't last long that first time, and Harvey elbowed his way back in. But then a year later she dropped Harvey and she and Nick were married."

"And you think Harvey carried a grudge all these years?"

I shrugged. "Made him look pretty bad."

Hendrickson flipped to a fresh page on his pad. "What about Harvey's badgering, how did Nick react to that?"

"Well, how would he? He hated it. Right from the start, Harvey tried to make Nick look bad in front of the board and other people on the job. Hell, he even badmouthed him at coffee row. To me that's downright dirty. I wouldn't have blamed Nick if he had taken a swing at Harvey."

"Do you think he did?" Hendrickson asked. "Do you think he took a swing at Kristoff?" He gave me a penetrating look, suggesting I give a truthful answer, and while I answered in the negative, I had to admit to some doubt.

That evening, over supper, I found myself wondering, could Nick have done this thing? I imagined a scene where the two meet at the seventh green to talk about the pink slip. Harvey starts railing on Nick, tells him he's no good, should have been fired ages ago and is glad to see he's out of there. Nick loses it, and in a fit of anger whaps Harvey over the head a few times.

"Bart, Bart..." I heard Rosie's voice. "Are you listening to me?"

"Yeah, of course I'm listening."

"Well anyway, Helen Mousie says her unofficial poll at the Co-op has it two to one that Nick did it."

"Oh, for Christ sake, how morbid."

"Yeah," Rosie said, "and what evidence is there against him anyway?"

"Some," I had to admit.

"What does that mean?"

"According to Hendrickson, if the prosecutor can prove that Nick was pissed-off enough at Harvey for firing him, that would be motive; Harvey was killed with a blunt object resembling a golf club, that's means..."

"Everybody's got golf clubs out there," Rosie said, "it's a golf course for pity sake."

"True, but legally it still constitutes means."

Rosie was unconvinced. But she hadn't sat across from Frank Hendrickson who had told me just how damning the evidence was. Only opportunity has yet to be established, were his final words.

As Rosie and I sat thinking our own thoughts, my mind drifted back, as it often did, to that day on the lake. Nick and I had skipped school and gone skating at Ireland's Point. There'd only been a light dusting of snow and the wind had blown that off leaving giant expanses of dark blue ice. Like walking on water, we were able to circumnavigate islands, sail up and down the shore or even risk the farthest reaches from land.

We naturally had our hockey sticks. Nick shot a hard one at me, and I missed it; the puck floated out further and further. Without thinking, I was after it. When I realized how far out I'd gone, it was too late. First I felt a thump, then there was cracking all around me, and finally a whumff as the ice gave way and the water swallowed me up. My body went into spasm as much from fear as from the freezing cold water. I remembered Nick racing towards me as I came up to the surface. I struggled to get out, but the ice kept breaking and I quickly grew weak in the punishingly cold water. When he reached me, Nick lay spread-eagled on the ice and began inching his way closer, extending his hockey stick towards me. I got hold of the stick and with thrashing and clinging and pulling and heaving, I was finally out and laying on the ice surface. We'd had a fire going earlier which we rekindled, and I was able to dry off enough to walk home. That's a day I will never forget, nor will I forget that Nick Taylor saved my life.

The phone rang.

"Hello, Mr. Bartowski?" a high-pitched voice queried.

"Yeah, this is Bart Bartowski."

"This is Ron Diccum. I'm the new greens keeper at the golf course," he said, making it sound like a question.

I looked over at Rosie, raised my eyebrows and made a frosty face at the receiver. "What can I do for you?"

"I just wanted to say hello. And since you're the only board member I haven't met, I thought perhaps we could sit down and have a little talk. I want to reassure you that I hope to continue with Nick's plans for the golf course, under the board's supervision, naturally," he added, breathing hard. "From what I've seen so far,

Nick's done a real good job and I only hope I can do as well."

I found myself warming up to Ron Diccum, despite the elevated pitch.

After a pause he said, "So, if you're free after supper, I wondered if we could meet at the Junction Stop."

"Sure, why not. How will I know you?" I asked.

"I don't think that'll be a problem," he said. "How's seven-thirty?"

"Fine."

The Junction Stop is a restaurant just out of town that takes advantage of the convergence of Highways Four and Thirty-seven and does a good business serving gas and heaping helpings of *home cooking*. Almost all the tables and booths were full. As I stood at the counter surveying the room, a giant of a man wearing a Crooked Lake golf cap struggled to stand up at a booth tucked in behind the waitress's station. He waved me over with a thrifty movement of his ham-like hand. His size became even more awesome the closer I got to him. When he reached out that ham bone to me, I must admit, I was a little afraid to take it.

"Ron Diccum," he said in that strange voice, pitched so high and delivered so softly that I had a hard time believing it came from this massive form.

"How do you do," I said, and slid into the booth across from him. As usual at the Junction Stop, a waitress appeared immediately, a pot of steaming coffee in hand. I waited for her to pour me a cup and clear a stack of supper dishes away from Ron Diccum's side of the table. "So, how do you like Crooked Lake?" I asked.

"It's great. I'm finding people friendly and I've got a real nice place to live. And you can't beat the food here," he added, waving his arm expansively, as if displaying his own personal larder.

"So, where did you work before you came to Crooked Lake?" I asked, and realized it sounded more like an interview question than a friendly inquiry.

"I ran the East End course for a couple of years," he said cooperatively, "then worked at the Crystal Creek Golf Club as assistant greens keeper. And before that, I was in the turf business. I sold turf for about ten years in Saskatoon."

"It's a good place to start greens keeping," I said.

The big man smiled uncomfortably. He seemed to be chewing on something, but appeared reluctant to spit it out.

"Something on your mind?" I asked.

He exhaled noisily. "Okay." He put his elbows on the table and linked his sausage-like fingers together. "I was at the boat launch eating an early supper around the time Mr. Kristoff was murdered." Ron Diccum looked at me as though I would interrupt, then he continued, "I had the small pair of binoculars I like to carry on the golf course to keep an eye on things. Anyway, I was eating my chicken and I was looking around just to see what I could see, when I spotted a small boat coming across the lake. What attracted my attention was that it was giving off a real good plume of blue smoke. But the odd thing was," and here the huge man shifted his eyes from side to side as though he didn't want to be overheard, "it was driven by a woman. She was dressed up real nice. I figured maybe she just arrived from the city and was heading for her cottage or something. She looked kinda out of place, handled the boat pretty good though. It wasn't until this morning that it came to me, there are no cottages on that part of the lake. Only thing there," he looked at me sheepishly, "is the seventh hole."

"Did you tell the police about it?"

"Well that's the point, eh? They must have talked to me for half an hour, first one, then the other. Detectives. I feel kind of foolish because I forgot all about seeing the boat," for a moment his gaze rested on a plump waitress standing at the table across from us," or maybe I didn't forget, just thought it wasn't important. But now, I'm not so sure."

"Had you seen it before?" I asked.

"Not that I can recall, and like I say, I forgot all about it. I finished my supper and went back to work. We had the keeper from P.A. looking at those two greens that were redone last year. We were over on number four when we heard the police siren coming down the hill."

"What time was that?" I asked.

"It was around five-thirty. I went straight over to number seven, almost as if I knew that's where they were going. Then the police shut down the course and nobody was allowed to leave. They were even keeping boaters from leaving the marina. They asked me to show them the tee-off time sheets. It was some guys from Sturgeon that found Mr. Kristoff. He was lying in the rough between the green and the lake. I guess one of the balls ended up right next to him." Ron looked a little queasy.

I thought it might be a good idea to get off that particular topic, since the big fella had just eaten. "I'm sure the police would want to know about that boat,

Ron. I imagine every detail is important when it comes to a murder investigation."

He moved his big body around uncomfortably, his shirt nearly popping buttons as it twisted tightly against his massive chest.

"By the way, what did she look like?" I asked.

"Who?"

"The woman in the boat."

"Oh," he said. "She was wearing a suit. You never see anybody driving a boat in a suit, eh?" Then his eyes grew wider, and his puffy face lifted. "It was a green suit, and she wore something over her head, an orange scarf, I think, and there were red bangs. Yeah, and she wore sunglasses, real dark ones." I watched the big man, waiting for more. "I'm going to take your advice," he said. "I'm going to talk to the police first thing in the morning." He squeezed out of the booth and struggling to his feet, extended his hand towards me. "I was told you were someone who would listen. Thank you, Bart, I'm real glad I was able to get that off my chest." Actually for such a giant his handshake was quite gentle; damp, but gentle. "I look forward to working with you," he added before lumbering off in the direction of the dessert buffet.

I meandered over to the Junction Stop Convenience Store and Bakery. They make a good cheese Danish there and sell locally-made smoked meats. I bought some of each. Driving home, I chewed on a fresh stick of Ukrainian sausage and the story the rotund Ron Diccum had just told me.

Picking up some Pepto-Bismol at the drugstore the next morning, I ran into Nettie Ostrowsky, the RCMP secretary. She told me that Ron Diccum had been into the detachment early that morning, and his statement had set off quite a flurry.

"Just between you, me and the fence post," Nettie said, "those detectives weren't real happy to hear about it. I think they're anxious to lay charges against Nick. But you still gotta ask who was that redhead?"

"What about Ellen Kristoff?" I said.

"What about her?"

"Where was she?"

Nettie looked at me as if I were one big, insensitive jerk. "Well, for one thing, she's no redhead and besides she was at home working in the garden, and there are plenty of witnesses to verify it." Nettie then turned on her heel and headed out the door, while I went to pay for my Pepto.

Despite these new revelations, Nick Taylor was formally charged with the murder of Harvey Kristoff that afternoon. By suppertime he'd already been locked up in the basement cells of the RCMP detachment. Rosie had learned this while delivering perogies and roasted sausage to the Taylor house.

Friends and neighbours often respond to crises with donations of food in small town Saskatchewan. I guess it's felt that the beleaguered family, being so distraught, is incapable of taking care of normal day-to-day chores, such as preparing meals. At the same time, a gift of nurturing food is a way of saying we are sorry for your trouble and we care about you, without actually having to say it.

The amount and type of food depends upon the calamity that has befallen a family. A death, being the worst, precipitates many days, if not weeks of casseroles, stews, big pots of homemade soup and so on, while a visit to the hospital will often fetch cookies, date squares or if you're not so lucky, fruit. Now an arrest for murder, not being a common family disaster, was more difficult to assess. According to Rosie, the result was mixed; everything from scalloped potatoes to devils food cake. The latter from Bill Bird, a retired English teacher.

"There was enough food for a wedding over there," Rosie said when she got back, "or a funeral. Wilma's mom was there, she just got outta the hospital yesterday, poor thing."

"How're the kids doing?"

"What do you think? Terrible. Wilma couldn't get Jake out of his room, and Susan was in tears. I pray that Nick isn't guilty, if only for their sake."

Harvey's Kristoff's funeral was held at eleven the following morning at St. Mary's Catholic Church. The closed casket stood at the front of the church and was adorned with a single bouquet of fresh lilies. Long-stemmed roses filled tall vases on either side of the casket and some green ivy peaked over the lip of the altar. By Crooked Lake standards, the arrangements would be considered austere, if not downright stark, but the formal simplicity seemed appropriate, given the circumstances.

Occupying the front row, nearest the casket was Ellen Kristoff, the widow. A dark veil concealed her face. Harvey's brother Carl sat next to her, along with two aged aunts who had been shipped from a Prince Albert rest home where they'd been in storage for a number of years. Behind them, filling an entire pew, the somber men of the Knights of Columbus sat in tribute to one of their own.

Rosie and I took our seats in the back row of the crammed church just before Father Lebret's call to worship hushed the large crowd. He began in a tenor singsong, "We are gathered together to mourn the loss of a member of this church who shared generously of both his time and his beneficence." There were some raised eyebrows among the mourners. "In the prime of his life, Harvey Kristoff was taken from his family, his friends and his community. And while judgment shall rain down on each and every one of us, he who plucked Harvey, unripened from the tree of life, will surely burn in hell fire for all eternity." The only response to his words was the creak of well-worn pews echoing through the porticoes of St. Mary's.

Carl Kristoff was then invited to the pulpit to eulogize his brother. Unlike Harvey, Carl had not succumbed to middle-aged spread; in fact in his charcoal gray suit, a slash of violet at his breast pocket and a matching tie, he looked quite fashionable. Rosie even detected a discreet blond streaking in his longish brown hair.

Carl, like Father Lebret, used the eulogy as much to demonize the killer as to document a life, well and fully lived. Nor did he leave any doubt as to whom he referred. "From where he sits in his cell, may he contemplate the harm that he has perpetrated upon this wife," Carl looked sorrowfully at Ellen, "and upon this family," and here he glanced at the aunts, one of whom had nodded off. "May he admit his guilt and thereby bring some small comfort to us, the bereaved." The large crowd stirred perceptibly.

At the conclusion of the service, the congregation watched as the pallbearers, including Les Thatcher and Lloyd Hughes, rolled the casket slowly down the centre aisle.

"Can you believe that?" I said to Rosie. "He as much as said Nick did it. What ever happened to innocent until proven guilty?"

She took my arm and whispered, "Let's not talk about it here."

I tried to say more, but she pinched the underside of my arm, hard.

Ellen Kristoff followed the pallbearers, escorted by Carl who kept a consoling hand at her elbow. She had married Harvey seven years before, then disappeared into the lake front house that Harvey had built at Grayham Point. The marriage had begun in tragedy when less than a year after the wedding, Ellen was crippled in a water skiing accident, leaving her with irreparable damage to her leg, and a pronounced limp. And now with the violent death of Harvey, the marriage had also ended in tragedy.

Rosie and I joined the queue that was forming to pay respects to the members of the funeral party. Ellen had swept her veil over her hat and looked quite regal as she accepted condolences; her eyes, though, showed the strain.

"I'm terribly sorry about Harvey," I said, feeling real sympathy for Ellen.

"Thank you." She smiled, belying nothing of what she must have been going through.

"I know that Harvey will be missed, he contributed a lot to this community."

"Yes," she said, "he contributed a lot," she leaned in closer, "and he demanded a lot too. Maybe too much for some people."

I imagined she referred to Nick and on his behalf felt behooved to say something, but I knew this wasn't the time or the place, so I said, "If you need anything, you let us know."

As she grasped Rosie's hand, she said, "I don't know what I'm going to do with that big house. I love gardening but…"

"There's plenty of time for that," Rosie said. "Right now it's time to say goodbye to Harvey."

"Yes, Harvey," Ellen said, as though she'd forgotten why she was there.

"He will be missed," Rosie added, dutifully. But Ellen had already turned to greet others in line.

Up close Carl Kristoff didn't look as good as he had in the pulpit. His face was sallow and his expression, though jovial, seemed just a little desperate.

"It's been a long time," I said.

"Too long," he said patting my shoulder sportingly.

"Where're you living these days, Carl?" Rosie asked.

"Oh, I've been in Mississauga for a long time."

"That's in Quebec, isn't it?" Rosie said.

"Ontario actually," Carl said, "near Toronto." I noticed a few impatient looks from down the line. "I'm kinda between places right now," he said, "my daughter is off to school in the States and I'm at loose ends, not sure where I'll end up."

"Well, it would be nice to have you back in Crooked Lake," Rosie said with genuine enthusiasm. Carl's reaction was lukewarm at best. After a few more words of condolence with the two aunts, who appeared to be tiring fast, Rosie and I returned home.

I got into my work boots and headed out to the shed that houses the garden tools and provides a home for our golden retriever. Along with my tools, I collected onions and seed potatoes. To my mind nothing heralds the promise of a good harvest like new potatoes smothered in butter and sprinkled with sweet green onions. I used my hoe to dig shallow holes into which I pressed halved seed potatoes, face down, eyes up. The soil below the surface was bone dry due to yet another rainless spring, so I flooded each divot with water.

As I worked, my mind turned over the events that had my friend's future twisted into a knot from which there seemed only one escape. That Nick was capable of murder was inconceivable, yet a niggling doubt poked at my resolve. Maybe it was something Carl Kristoff had said or the look on Ellen Kristoff's face. But soon these thoughts were displaced by the task at hand, and I buried another seed potato in the dark earth.

4

The cells at the RCMP detachment were used mainly for DWI's, D & D's and short term incarcerations. Three cells along one wall faced a guard station, making them secure without being overly oppressive and the walls displayed only a modicum of graffiti, none too obscene.

A young constable patted me down before I was allowed into Nick's cell. Nick was sitting at a small wooden table with a copy of *the Star Phoenix* laid out in front of him. I noticed he wore no belt and the laces had been removed from his shoes. The irony was that one of his off-season jobs had been to watch prisoners in the very guard station across from which he now sat.

"What's new?" I said, nodding towards the paper.

I sat down across from him while he riffled through it. "Have a look at this," he said, pushing the paper towards me.

The headline read, *Murder in Crooked Lake*. There was a picture of Nick next to the article. "That's a hockey picture for Christ sake," he said. It showed Nick after a game, disheveled, a cut above one eye and looking a little deranged.

"I remember that game," I said, "playoffs against Maidstone, right?"

The article described the brutal murder and depicted Nick as the only suspect. "What a lot of horseshit," he said, as he tossed the paper aside. "I think the cops just want to hang this on somebody, and I'm easy picking's."

"Speaking of picking's," I said, "I brought some of Rosie's Saskatoon berry pie." I didn't add, *to cheer you up*, but I hoped it would. I pulled two slices out of a thermal lunch bag. The pie was still warm and Rosie had even whipped some cream to go with it. Nick took a generous bite, chewed and washed it down with coffee from a styrofoam cup.

"What does your lawyer have to say?" I asked.

His look said that Hendrickson hadn't had much to say. He chewed some more, then attempted to wipe whipped cream out of his luxuriant mustache. "He did a good job for Wilma's brother," Nick said.

"On a boundary dispute," I reminded him.

"I know, but what am I supposed to do? I don't know any lawyers." The constable that had searched me earlier ushered a rumpled overnighter out of the cellblock.

"Why don't you see how the preliminary goes tomorrow?" I said. "Then you can decide."

He nodded indifferently.

When we'd run out of things to talk about, I shuffled a well-worn deck of cards that lay on the wooden table. "How about a little pinochle?" I said.

"Why not," he said, "I'm not going anywhere."

The following morning, Doc and I drove into Saskatoon to attend Nick's preliminary hearing. The sky had turned an angry gray. The dark clouds would raise hopes for rain, though years of drought had left most farmers doubting whether they'd ever see a good crop again.

As he gazed over the bald countryside, Doc said, "You know, Nick wasn't doing such a bad job."

"So, why'd you vote against him?"

Doc shook his head. "I didn't. But I didn't speak out for him either, and I wish I had. But Harvey kept pushing. It was bad enough at board meetings, but every time I'd see him he'd have at least one gripe about Nick. I guess it influenced me." Doc turned to the window. "I don't blame Nick."

The speedometer had crept up to seventy mph. I checked my rear view mirror. "Blame him for what? You don't seriously believe he'd kill a guy over a job, do you?"

He remained unspecific and non-committal, much like a doctor giving a prognosis.

In a little over an hour we had reached Saskatoon. We drove over the University Bridge and though it was May, the river below still carried snow-encrusted chunks of ice down stream. A few minutes later we entered the provincial courthouse, one of the city's grand edifices, built when the country was young and still optimistic.

Nick, wearing a suit, sat next to Frank Hendrickson. Wilma, her shapely legs emerging from a short skirt, sat directly behind them with her mother and sister.

"All rise," the court clerk announced as the robed judge entered. "Hear ye, hear ye, all those having an interest in these matters gather round, Judge Richard Kaleniuk presiding."

Judge Kaleniuk addressed the court. He was a tall, distinguished looking man of about fifty. I'd read that he'd made his reputation as a tireless legal aid attorney before recently being promoted to the bench. "In the matter of the Province of Saskatchewan versus Nick

Taylor," he said. "Mr. Taylor, you stand accused of first degree murder." Doc and I exchanged glances. "Do you understand the charge?"

"Yes," Nick responded.

"How do you plead?"

Nick and his lawyer stood. Frank Hendrickson said, "Your Honour, my client pleads not guilty to the charge."

"So noted," Judge Kaleniuk responded.

"Furthermore, Your Honour," Hendrickson said, "defense requests a transfer to Court of Queens Bench where we will prove that the Crown has insufficient evidence with which to proceed."

"I've looked over the evidence and I disagree," the judge said, "however, I will consider your request. As to the matter of bail."

The Crown attorney shot to his feet. "Your Honour, the Crown requests bail in the amount of one hundred thousand dollars. And further requests that Your Honour set an early trial date, as staff holidays would likely interfere with a summer trial."

"You mean," Judge Kaleniuk countered," a summer trial would interfere with staff holidays." Looking uncomfortable, the prosecuting attorney made a gesture of concurrence.

Judge Kaleniuk looked over some papers he had in front of him. All but the court clerk gazed at the judge. "Mr. Taylor, I see you are married and have two children?"

Nick cleared his throat. "That's right, uh sir, I have a son and a daughter."

"And your wife works?"

At Frank Hendrickson's urging, Nick got to his feet. "Yes, she works at SaskTel in P.A."

"And you, Mr. Taylor?"

"I'm out of a job right now."

"So you would be looking after the children?"

"Well..." Frank Hendrickson whispered into Nick's ear. Nick cleared his throat and said, "Yes, I would be, Your Honour."

"Very well," Judge Kaleniuk said, writing a few notes. "Set bail at... twenty-five thousand dollars."

"But, Your Honour," the prosecutor protested, "the evidence emphatically implicates the accused..."

"The Crown's evidence," Hendrickson said, standing, "will not hold up under scrutiny, Your Honour."

"The nature of the crime, and the brutality with which it was carried out point to a strong possibility of flight," retorted the prosecutor.

"But His Honour has already noted that Mr. Taylor is a family man and the likelihood of flight is minimal to non-existent."

"To be perfectly honest, Your Honour," the prosecutor said, "we would prefer that the accused be kept in custody."

"Then you shouldn't have suggested that he be released on bail," Judge Kaleniuk said. He set the trial date and cautioned the advocates not to try the case in the press.

"All rise," the court clerk declared.

"The judge was definitely on your side," Hendrickson said, closing his briefcase with a snap.

"Think so?" Nick said. Wilma stood next to him, a pained expression on her face.

"Nick, I hope everything works out," Doc said. "And I'm sorry if anything I did added to your troubles."

"Don't worry about it, Doc."

"We better go take care of the paper work and get you out of here," Hendrickson said. An officer of the court stood by.

Outside the courthouse I watched Carl Kristoff cross the street and hop into Harvey's SUV. He'd no doubt been sitting behind us in the courtroom.

On the drive back to Crooked Lake I thought about what the prosecutor had said—the nature and brutality of the crime. There was little doubt that it was brutal. According to rumours, Harvey's head and face were bashed in beyond recognition. It wasn't until the police checked his wallet that they confirmed it was, in fact, Harvey. "To me that's more than just doing a guy in, eh," I said to Doc, "it's like trying to pummel him out of existence."

The clouds had dissipated and the wind had picked up, again disappointing farmers' hopes for rain. After dropping Doc off at the clinic, I stopped in to see Fred Snell. I hoped to learn a little about this "emphatically indicating" evidence that the prosecutor had alluded to.

"Bart, I can't really tell you much," Fred said when he realized I was fishing for information.

"Why all the secrecy, Fred? All I want to know is why you think Nick's guilty of murder?"

"I don't think he's guilty of murder. That's not my job. We simply find facts and present them to the Crown. The Crown decides whether to pursue it further."

"Okay, so tell me some of these facts."

"Bart, I'm really not at liberty to divulge information to the general public," Fred said in his *by-the-book* voice.

"I'm not the general public, Fred, I'm the big defenseman who rang your bell at the last old-timers' game, remember?"

His eyes strayed to the outer office. All was quiet. "What the hell." He got up and closed the door, then he loosened his tie. "Besides having no alibi, there's one major piece of evidence."

"And what's that?" I asked.

"Nick's seven iron was found with traces of blood on it, even hair stuck to it."

"Good Lord."

"In his bag."

"In his golf bag? Who would be stupid enough to leave something like that in his own bag?"

"There were no other fingerprints on it except Nick's." Fred leaned back in his chair, crossed his arms and shrugged.

"What else?" I said.

"What more do you want?"

"Isn't there any evidence that points to Nick's innocence?"

"That's not how it works."

"Wait. Let me get this straight. There's you guys and your city detectives and a bunch of prosecutors out to prove Nick guilty. And then there's one little property lawyer up in P.A. trying to prove he's innocent. You know, Fred, that just doesn't seem fair."

"Maybe not, but that's how it works and there's nothing you can do about it."

Nothing you can do about it. Those words stuck in my craw. Stepping out of the station I spotted Nettie, the detachment secretary, hustling around the corner of the building towards me. She held a sweater tightly around her, trying to keep out the brisk spring breeze. She took a furtive glance at the door, then in a conspiratorial tone said, "There's one thing he probably didn't tell you, Bart."

"What was that?" I asked.

"Well, Harvey was having a little, you know," she raised her eyebrows in a suggestive manner, "dessert on the side."

Harvey wasn't particularly known for his monogamy and in a town the size of Crooked Lake, it was hard to keep things like that secret.

"And who do you think his little dish was?" Nettie smiled deliciously.

"Who?" I said.

"Wilma Taylor."

I felt my jaw drop. "You can't be serious?"

"They must have rekindled the old flame," Nettie said. "It was an anonymous tip." She nodded towards the door. "They've been trying to keep it quiet." Fred had certainly done that.

"So they think Nick did it because of that?" I said.

"That's one possibility."

"What do you mean? What other possibility is there?"

"Well," Nettie said coyly, "Wilma's a redhead. Put two and two together."

"What, they think she was the redhead in the boat? You can't be serious." I thought about it for a moment. "Anyway, she was visiting her mother in the hospital, forty miles away."

"It's not an airtight alibi," Nettie said sagely. "Her mother was asleep and no one saw Wilma leave." Then

Nettie added poignantly, "We'll have to see how her story stands up, won't we? They're bringing her in soon as she gets back from work."

"Wilma," Rosie made one of her commingled faces, not believing, yet not disbelieving either, "and Harvey? What could she possibly see in Harvey?"

"Maybe the same thing she saw in him back in high school," I said.

"But, good grief, a lot has changed since then."

Harvey had become stocky, balding, and a little bow-legged since he'd courted Wilma in high school, but apparently he was not entirely unbearable. In fact ever since Roberta Kovacs had let slip that Harvey was especially well endowed—and she'd been in a position to know—there had been a certain lewd mystique about him. Besides, what he lacked in personal appeal, he more than made up for with his confident bearing and bags of money. Harvey had bought the AgrowChem franchise just as farming was becoming big business, and along with the income from his land rental and Kristoff Realty, he'd become one of the wealthiest men in Crooked Lake.

Now as I said, Wilma did not lack attributes. In the old-timers' best-female-parts pool, an informal and, we liked to think, benign objectification of Crooked Lake's gentler sex, Wilma always came in Miss Best Legs. What's more, she had silky red hair with bangs that danced playfully off long eyelashes above alluring amber eyes. And even though she'd put on a few pounds and "weren't no spring chicken", Wilma could still bring the boys to attention when she walked into a room.

"Do you think Nick found out about her and Harvey?" Rosie wondered. "If Nick knew about it, then getting fired was probably the last straw. He couldn't take it anymore, so he went out and confronted Harvey." Rosie filled many a long winter night curled up with paperback murder mysteries.

In response to my skeptical look, she said, "Well, Nick could have done it. I mean let's face it, Harvey was an unlikable jerk, and he made life pretty miserable for Nick."

I had to agree with her there.

"And you know Nick, he likes his liquor—Rosie's favourite explanation for all the problems of the world—and when people drink, they don't think rationally, in fact sometimes they don't think at all. I know that they do things they wouldn't do sober." And *you're no exception* her look said. "The gentlest lambs on earth can turn into beasts when they're drunk. And do you know where Nick was at dinnertime, the day of the murder?"

"Where?"

"At the pub, tossin' back a few."

"According to who?" I said.

She just looked smug.

"I don't buy it, Rosie. Sure, Nick may be a scrappy guy, but he's never resorted to violence to solve his problems, and I'm damn sure he didn't this time either."

"Yeah, prove it," Rosie challenged.

I just might, I thought to myself, I just might do that.

Next morning I had a long-distance conversation with my booking agent, Raulley, down in Dallas, Texas.

"It's going to be a good year, Bart. I've already had to turn customers away."

"Really?"

"If things keep going at this pace, we could book the lodge twice over this summer."

"Jesus, maybe I should build that new cabin we talked about."

"You'd cover the cost in no time," he said.

"Yeah, but Rosie would never agree, given our unpredictable future."

"What's the news on that front?" Raulley asked.

"No news, except what they've already told us. We've been talking to some young twerp down in Regina. The department is busy with gold and diamonds, so our appeal is on the back burner, he said. I'd like to put him on the back burner. Anyway, no change, the lease expires on December thirty-first."

"I hope things work out, Bart," Raulley said in his Texas drawl. "I've got a lot of fishermen that'll be sorely disappointed if your lodge shuts down."

"They're not the only ones who'll be disappointed," I said. As I re-cradled the phone, I noticed Rosie standing in the doorway to my office, eyes blazing. Stepping around my desk, I said, "We're going to beat this thing, Rosie, I know it." I reached out to touch her, but she drew away.

Neither of us could imagine a future without Stuart Lake Lodge. For over fifteen years we'd been working hard, developing the business and cultivating a loyal clientele. But all our hard work was now in jeopardy. A mining company had recently discovered diamonds nearby and had applied for an exploration lease that would cover hundreds of square miles, including Stuart

Lake. The government would receive huge revenues if and when a mine went into production. And just like that, we were given notice that our lease, which would expire in December, would not be renewed.

But there was no point to this conversation. Rosie and I had been through it dozens of times and it always ended the same. We had no influence over a financially beleaguered government that saw dollar signs every time it looked at Capex International's proposal.

"I'll ignore your bizarre suggestion that we build a new cabin," Rosie said stiffly, "and besides, we've got enough work to do around there. Too much sometimes. I've been talking to Myra and she says I'm crazy to do it all by myself." Myra is Rosie's opinionated sister.

"I help, don't I?" I said, a little hurt.

"Anyway, I've hired the young Babich girl to work in the kitchen."

"You what?"

"We can see how it works out," Rosie persisted. "Her mum tells me she's a hard working girl and apparently she's a fisherman too."

"We usually discuss things like this, honey," I said.

"Yeah well, there's no point breaking our backs, is there?"

She was right about that. And if this kid liked to fish, so much the better.

"Any other surprises up your sleeve?" I said. Rosie lowered herself into a chair and stared at one of the pictures on my office wall, the one of her and me with a young Charlie Mackenzie. "If not," I said, "I'm gonna head over to the marine shop and check on those outboards." The picture had been taken on our new dock. We'd all been smiling into the camera. It was opening day of our first year in business.

As I put away a few things that lay on the desk, the phone rang. I picked up and was pleased to hear our daughter's voice. "Hi Annie." I motioned to Rosie. "How's everything?"

"Fine," she said, a note of uncertainty in her voice.

"Classes okay?" I said. Annie was taking environmental studies at the University of Saskatchewan in Saskatoon.

"Not as interesting as last semester."

"You coming home soon?"

"Yeah, I am."

"She's coming home," I whispered to Rosie, who despite her earlier mood, softened upon hearing the news.

"And I'm bringing Randall."

"Oh, that's great," I said with more enthusiasm than I felt. She'd been seeing Randall, a fellow environmental student, for almost a year. He was a nice enough kid, I just thought they were getting a little too serious. At only twenty, I wanted Annie to keep her options open. "When are you coming?"

"We'll be there Saturday morning sometime," she said. Where would they be Friday night, I wondered?

"Mom would like to say hello," I said in response to Rosie's waving.

I took Butch on his daily jaunt down cemetery road. He mostly runs in and out of the deep ditches and makes long forays into the fields on either side of the road. Crooked Lake rests in the Potato River basin, just a half mile from the western extremity of the lake. The town had begun right on the shore, but some shenanigans with the location of the railroad forced a slight change of venue.

Nevertheless, Crooked Lake is a pretty little town with tree-lined streets, well kept homes, a great school, skating rink and even comfortable retirement residences for the elderly. The quality of life here is second to none in my book. You can have your big city sophistication; as far as I'm concerned it comes at too high a price. All I hear from city folk are complaints about congestion, pollution and crime. We've got no congestion, no pollution, and we've never once felt uncomfortable letting our kids go anywhere in this town, day or night.

In mid-thought I remembered, someone in our pretty little, tree-lined town had been murdered a few days ago. I wondered if that act would undermine forever the complacent certainty that our community was safe?

Over at Northern Sales and Marine, I found my three 20-horse Evinrude's sitting on the workbench in pieces. The owner, Benny Langthorne, was nowhere to be seen. His helper stepped out of the office, sandwich in hand.

"Where's Benny?" I asked.

"He's working on the police boat out at Lasko Beach."

"What about my motors?" I asked.

"I don't know, you'll have to talk to Benny about that." The young man hunched his shoulders and took a giant size bite of his sandwich, effectively ending the conversation.

And my motors? I guess they would just sit there on the bench in pieces for a while longer. I decided to go over to Nick's and see how he was holding up.

When he answered the back door, the first thing he said was, "Care for a brew?" When I said it was a little early, he cracked one for himself and we sat down in the living room where a couple of dead soldiers had already tumbled over on the coffee table.

"How are you doing?" I said.

"Whaddaya think?" He chased the despondent look off his face with a long pull from his beer. "At least I'm not locked up," he said.

I nodded my head. "What about Wilma?" I asked. "Did the police check out her alibi?"

"Yeah. She was still in P.A. when it happened; had a gas receipt to prove it."

Again I nodded my head. "That's good news."

"Can you believe this?" he said miserably. "We're both suspected of murder. And what about Jake and Susan? Imagine what they're going through, everybody in town treating them like dog shit. As if all this was their fault. Sometimes I just don't know what I'm going to..." All at once Nick's face contorted and his eyes closed. He took his head in his hands. His breath came in gasps. He tried to hold back but when the dam burst, he cried long and hard. I went and sat down next to him on the couch and put an arm around his shuddering shoulders. When he had run out of tears, he wiped his eyes with the sleeve of his shirt and slowly shook his head from side to side. He put his hand on my jean-clad knee and said in a trembling voice, "You're a good friend, Bart." He turned and looked directly at me for the first time since I'd come in. "You know I didn't do it, eh?"

I hesitated and looked at his tormented face. A face I'd known my entire life. I'd watched Nick grow from a boy to a man, even stood up for him at his wedding.

"You do believe me, don't you?"

"Of course," I said.

"'Cause if you didn't..." his eyes began to well up again.

"I believe you, Nick."

He took a deep breath and visibly relaxed. "What do you think my chances are?" he said, his voice still a little shaky.

This was definitely a time for one of my famous old-timers' pep talks, the one I usually give just before the start of the third period when we're down ten - zip.

Nick could see me gearing up for it and cut me off with, "No bullshit."

I took a deep breath and organized my thoughts. "Okay," I said, "no bullshit."

Nick lowered his eyes and took another swig off his bottle of *Pil.*

"Well, no question, there are a few things against you," I said. "Like no alibi."

"I just drove around, trying to clear my head," he said. "I admit it, I was goddamned pissed off. And yes, I was pissed off at Harvey. I just needed to get away for a while."

"You didn't see anybody?"

"Hell, I was on country roads, there's nobody for miles around out there."

"Then there's your seven iron," I said, "and that's one hell of a piece of evidence."

"Yeah," he said.

"What about it?"

"Fucked if I know," he barked. "I picked up my clubs from the pro-shop, where I've always kept them, eh. I just grabbed the bag and threw it in the back seat. When

I got home I shoved it in the shed where we store Wilma's clubs, and the kids' too."

"Do you lock the shed?"

"Nah, what for? Maybe when we go away for a few days, but not when we're around town." He leaned forward. "What? You think somebody got at my clubs in there?"

"Could be. Either there, or at the pro-shop."

He pulled at his bushy moustache. "But who for Christ sake?"

"That's the question, I guess. Do you remember if the seven iron was in your bag when you picked it up from the pro-shop?"

"No. No idea."

"Because somebody could have taken it from there, used it to kill Harvey, then returned it to your bag in the shed." The seven iron is the heaviest club in the bag, which makes it an ideal choice for a murder weapon.

He tapped his bottle on the table rhythmically. "What else is there?"

It felt like hell, but I owed it to my friend. "There's the Wilma - Harvey thing."

Nick's blue eyes iced over.

"It's a strong motive, one of the strongest, Hendrickson says."

"I didn't know," Nick protested. He shook his head in despair. "When that prick Klassen asked me about it, I just about hit him. I was sure he was just trying to get my goat." Nick clutched his beer bottle and inhaled deeply, as if to ward off breaking down again.

Neither of us spoke. St. Mary's bell tolled, indicating twelve noon and mercifully interrupting what seemed an interminable silence.

"Guess the kids will be home for dinner soon," I said, a little relieved.

Nick got up unsteadily and headed for the kitchen. Though he'd given it up years earlier, he said, "Christ, I could sure use a smoke right now."

5

Crooked Lake is a long snaking expanse of water about two miles wide and fifteen miles long. Near the source at the marshy mouth of the Potato River is the all but abandoned, Lasko Beach.

I spotted Benny Langthorne down at the main dock. His van was backed in, giving him easy access to his tools. "Hey Benny, how's it going?"

He looked up from where he knelt over the big engine at the rear of the police boat. "Bart," he said in a beleaguered tone, "what brings you out here?"

"Oh I had nothing to do, so I thought I'd take a ride. How's it going?"

"Slow, very slow. They banged this thing up pretty good. I really should have it in the shop, but they're looking for a quick fix so they can get back out on the lake." He straightened up stiffly and reached for a wrench. "I suppose you're wondering about your motors."

"Well, my season starts soon, eh."

"I'll get to them as soon as this thing's done," Benny said, twisting himself pretzel-like and applying the wrench to a small nut.

I looked around Lasko Beach. The old pavilion, where in its heyday people would gather for Saturday night dances, weddings and the like, was now condemned and stood awaiting demolition, part of the roof already collapsed. The original owner of the land, Mike Lasko, was long-since dead.

Encroaching on the beach was a marshland of several hundred acres. Its burgeoning mosquito population had ultimately killed the resort, returning the area to a huge diversity of waterfowl. Annie had spent a lot of time at Lasko, her specialty being wetland birds, in fact *Ducks Unlimited* wanted to designate it a bird sanctuary.

As I panned the expansive marshland, I watched a young couple paddling a canoe not far from the beach. From the sound of things, he was giving a lesson that she was not absorbing as quickly as he would have liked. As I gazed about, I became aware of a reflective bobbing out in the marsh. Lowering my sunglasses from their perch on top of my head, I was able to make out what looked like an aluminum boat floating amongst the reeds.

"Looks like there's a boat out in the marsh," I said to Benny.

"Another amateur."

"What do you mean?"

"Why do you think I'm fixing this thing? They got too close and hit bottom. These young cops don't know squat about boating. Amateurs," he scoffed.

"Why do you suppose there's a boat out there then?"

"I don't know," he said with a grimace as he reefed on the stubborn nut. "There are a few deeper channels, but you've got to know exactly where they are. A rowboat's no problem if you can stand the mosquitoes."

I kept an eye on the shiny reflection of the boat. Benny struggled with the nut.

I hailed the young couple who now seemed to be drifting aimlessly about fifty yards off shore. "There's a boat out in the marsh," I said, "I wonder if you could give me a lift out there?"

The young man said," Sure." The young lady appeared not so willing.

An argument wafted over the water for a few moments before they began paddling raggedly towards the beach. The girl hauled her lithe form out of the canoe. "You can go with the Professor," she said, referring to the bespectacled twenty-something that occupied the canoe's stern.

I climbed into the small forward seat and took the paddle from the girl, giving her an understanding smile. The Professor and I pulled towards the marsh; he was a strong paddler and we quickly came along side the 12-foot aluminum boat. We tried unsuccessfully to dislodge it, the motor appeared to be grounded on a small islet of mud and weeds. I climbed gingerly out of the canoe and into the boat, just managing to stay on my feet. By rocking the motor I was able to raise the shaft out of the water. Then using the paddle, I shoved off and the boat floated free.

I reached down the shaft and wrestled with the long, muddy reeds that had wrapped themselves around the propeller. When they were clear, I pumped on the gas bulb and pulled sharply on the starter cord. The motor hiccupped a couple of times, then reluctantly began to fire more or less evenly. Putting it in gear, I pointed it towards the shore. I felt pebbles grating on the aluminum flooring under my feet as I steered toward the dock where Benny was working. At a moderate speed the motor ran quite smoothly, but left in its wake a thick plume of blue smoke.

I drove my truck towards Pebble Beach with the colourful stones that I'd found on the floor of the boat rattling around in my ashtray. Pebble Beach is the only shoreline on the lake that is pebbly, the others being mostly rocks, sand or face-slapping gooseberry bushes. At the access lane I slowed to a crawl, reading the signs that traditionally adorned lake cabins, monikers like: Foaker's Smoker, La Feat's Retreat, and Weakes' End. You get the idea.

After passing a few dozen lifeless cottages, I came to one with a shiny blue sports car parked in the drive. Burned into a varnished round of oak was the name Riskowsky's Housky. Okay, so they can't all be cute. I pulled over, nestling the side of my truck into the bushy willows that line the narrow lane. I walked down the shaded driveway, passing flowerbeds that waited for bulbs to burst forth and for annuals to be planted. There was a mature Weeping Birch at the centre of the lawn and some low-lying evergreens up against the cottage. There weren't many cottage owners who put this much effort into landscaping. I guess they got enough of it at home.

I reached the front of the cottage where the deck rested directly on the beach. An undue rise in the water level had been disastrous some years, but, with yet another dry spring, this wasn't one of those.

I squatted down and compared the pebbles I'd found in the bottom of the boat with those on the beach. They were an exact match, just as I thought.

As I examined the stones a female voice called out, "Hello, can I help you?"

A young couple in swimsuits sat on the deck on a beach blanket. He was a blond California type and she wasn't at all hard to look at. The young man, noticing my appreciative glance, placed his arm proprietarily around her curvy hip.

I tucked the pebbles into my pocket. "Sorry to barge in on you," I said. "I'm looking for the owner of a small aluminum boat, a 12-footer. The motor gives off quite a mess of smoke." I smiled.

"That could be the Riley's boat," the young woman said. "Their old outboard stinks to high heaven."

"Do you know if they're over there?"

"I doubt it." She wrinkled her nose appealingly. "Actually the Rileys haven't been out much in the last couple of years."

"Which cottage is theirs?" I asked.

"The third one over," she replied pointing down the beach.

"Well, thanks. And sorry to bust in on you like that." The young man looked pleased that I was leaving, even managed a crooked grin.

"No problem," the young woman said, her smile genuine. "Your name is Bartowski, right?"

"Bart. That's right," I said, a little surprised. "How'd you know?"

"We golfed in the same tournament a couple years ago," she said. "Your partner was a pretty blond, as I recall. I was golfing with my dad."

The young man's frown had returned.

"I'm Juliette Riskowsky." I picked up the scent of skin and coconut oil as she reached over the railing of the deck to shake my hand. "This is my friend Josh." Josh gave me a limp wave. "Would you care for a beer?" Juliette asked.

I knew Josh wouldn't be happy, so I said, "Sure, why not."

"Josh, would you mind getting Bart a beer?" He got up slowly, pulled open the screen door and disappeared inside.

Juliette moved a deck chair toward me. "So, what was it you wanted to talk to the Rileys about?"

"We're trying to discourage polluters," I lied, "and I wanted to talk to them about that motor."

She sat down on the colourful beach blanket and adjusted her bikini top. I tried not to stare, without much success, and naturally it was just then that Josh came out the screen door, carrying three Canadians. He passed one to me, along with a defiant glare, then took up his position on the blanket next to Juliette.

I guzzled some beer, then asked, "So, have you been out for a while?"

Pushing thick, dark hair off her forehead with splayed fingers, Juliette said, "We just arrived yesterday. Gosh, it's good to be here, though, especially now, when there aren't a lot people around."

I liked that she used the word, gosh. "So, you haven't seen anyone around?"

She turned to Josh. "Did you see anybody this morning?"

"No," he said, "we were in bed pretty late, remember?" He nudged her with his elbow. Juliette looked embarrassed.

"So, you're a golfer, are you?" Josh said.

"Yup," I said.

"What's your handicap?"

"Well, you got me there," I said, "but I usually shoot somewhere between thirty-five and forty on our nine-hole course."

"Wow, that's like seventy on eighteen holes," Juliette said. "Pretty impressive." Josh just raised his eyebrows and looked away.

I tossed back the rest of my beer. "I don't want to impose on you any longer," I said and got up to leave.

"If you're back this way, do stop by," Juliette said, standing and brushing at some non-existent sand on her taut belly. "The beer is always cold." As she offered her hand, I noticed she was just about as tall as me.

I walked a little further down the lane, to where a knotty slice of shellacked pine displayed the name, Riley's Rest. A new car was nestled, like mine, into the willows down the road a ways, but Riley's driveway was empty and the place had the same uninhabited look as most of the other cottages. It was a square, one-story building with factory aluminum windows and the popular oxblood stain preferred by cottage owners in these parts. I peered through one of the windows facing the lane, but a curtain blocked the view. Going around to the waterside, I saw a dock and a boathouse that had both seen better days. I decided to knock on the door, just in case the Rileys were *living the life*. Receiving no response, I tried the handle. The door came open with only slight resistance.

Now I was in new territory. Would this be considered breaking and entering? In reality, I wasn't breaking, but only entering. I wondered if there was a distinction. I decided there was, and stepped into the cottage.

The place looked lived-in. Dishes were stacked in doorless cabinets, towels hung to dry and the floor swept. Everything was wiped down and ship shape. The chrome kitchen table held several pens, a writing tablet and some envelopes. The only evident disorder was some crumpled paper strewn about the wastebasket under the table. I uncrumpled a sheet. It contained a bunch of calculations, calculations in the millions. I dug into the wastebasket itself, intrigued by what else I might find in this far from abandoned cottage. A stained, legal-size sheet turned out to be a job application form for the Regional Park. I wondered if the Rileys had a son who was looking for a summer job.

I wiped fresh banana peel off my hands and turned my attention to the bedrooms. The first was empty except for a large beach ball and some other stuff I couldn't really see in the dark room. The second bedroom was also shadowy, and when I flipped on the light switch, nothing happened. I went over to the window and drew the faded curtains aside. The room contained a double bed, neatly made, a dresser and a large chest of drawers upon which sat a few men's toiletries. Light from the window now streamed in, illuminating a worn suitcase on the closet floor. Attached to the handle was a leather I.D. label. I bent to read it when…a curious darkness oozed in all around me. It felt neither good nor bad, like going under anesthetic; though in this instance, I didn't get the option of counting backward. Just as the lights went out, my mind took a little trip of its own.

I saw Gran, her cheek against the side of her favourite Jersey…milk hissing into a metal can. Then I was in my attic bedroom, asleep. It was cold and still dark. Uncle Rudy was calling me. There were other men, all sitting around the large table in the kitchen.

One of them looked like my father and sitting next to him was somebody that looked a lot like Harvey Kristoff, but before long, everything turned to black once again.

6

A faint glow emanated from somewhere deep within. I gradually became aware of things around me and was able to make out vague shapes. I heard a voice, echoing and unintelligible, people conversing in urgent tones, the shuffle of feet, the clink and clang of instruments.

"He's waking up, Doctor," someone said.

I sensed movement in front of my face. "Can you see my hand?" a male voice inquired. Apparently satisfied with my response, he said, "Rosie is here and Stuart. Can you say hello to them?"

I said hello as clearly as I could. I heard Rosie sniffle.

"Dad, it's day light in the swamp, the roosters are crowing," Stuart mimicked my morning prattle.

I tried to smile, but when I heard Rosie's sniffle turn into a full-fledged sob, I realized I hadn't succeeded that well.

"Okay, Bart," I now recognized Doc Chow's voice, "you've been unconscious for a while, but you're going to be fine. I just want you to relax. It's going to take some time before all of your faculties return to good working order." I tuned out as Doc's voice went on making comforting sounds, plugging back in when I heard him say, "Is there anything you want right now, Bart? Anything you need?"

"Thirsty," I croaked. A straw was stuck between my dry lips and I sucked up some ginger ale, the elixir of the gods. I sucked some more, then returned to the dark place from whence I'd come. Grandpa wasn't at the table—he'd already died, they told me, kicked by a horse.

The next time I opened my eyes I had to close them against the bright light that flooded the room. I opened them again, warily this time, and could make out objects. A sink, a stack of towels, an open closet containing what looked like my gaudy bathrobe from home.

Rosie was sitting next to the bed, her head resting on the back of the chair. Her eyes were closed. A blanket of sunshine covered her. She looked like an angel sitting there, albeit a snoring angel.

Doc Chow walked in at that moment. Taking in the scene, he put his index finger up to his lips and said quietly, "She's been here all night, let's let her sleep. How're you feeling?" He leaned down close; I could smell toothpaste on his breath and see the tiny hairs in his nose.

I shook my head trying to clear it a little. "What the hell happened?"

"Let's talk about that later," Doc said. "Right now I want you to concentrate on getting better, getting your strength back. I'd like you to do a little experiment with me, okay?"

"Sure, why not."

"Let your mind focus on each part of your body and see if everything's working. First, I want you to move your left foot."

I focused on my foot, which seemed a long way off, and twisted "Good. Now your right. Your leg, knees, hands, arms. It looks like everything's working." I noticed that Rosie was awake and watching my movements with great anticipation.

I said, "I wonder if the most important part still works, Doc?"

"Oh, Bart." Rosie came over and gave me a tender kiss on the cheek.

"I think it's time you tried to eat something," Doc said. "Would you like a little breakfast?"

"How about bacon and eggs?" I suggested.

Doc twisted his head regretfully. "I think you'll have to settle for good old hospital gruel right now, Bart, but before long I'm sure you'll be clogging up your arteries with all sorts of good stuff." Rosie smiled broadly. I tried to smile too, but my face refused to cooperate.

The following morning as I tried to get my eyes to focus enough to read the *Crooked Lake Reporter*, I caught sight of Fred Snell standing in the doorway.

He wore street clothes and a sympathetic grin. "Hello, Bart, how're you feeling?"

"Oh, just wonderful, Fred."

He took a few steps into the room. "Doc says things are looking pretty good."

"Yeah." Though it felt like somebody was hitting me over the head with a hammer from time to time.

I noticed Doc hovering in the background as Fred asked, "Do you feel up to answering a few questions?"

"As long as you don't ask any hard ones," I said.

"I can't promise you that." He put one hand in the pocket of his jeans and the other on the bedrail. "What can you tell me about the accident?"

"What accident?"

Fred looked over at Doc. "Well," he spoke more slowly and louder than before, "you rolled your truck."

"What?"

"Some kids on bikes found you out at Ireland's Ravine. You must have lost control on that loose gravel."

"I did?" I didn't remember driving anywhere near Ireland's Ravine, and I certainly didn't remember rolling my truck.

Again I noticed Fred look over at Doc, who now stood on the other side of the bed. "Memory loss is not uncommon in cases like this," he said to Fred. "A good sharp knock on the head can do it."

I began to feel feverish. "I never rolled my truck."

"Then how did you wind up at the bottom of that ravine, in your truck, wheels pointing straight up?" Fred asked.

"I don't know," I said as much to myself as to him.

"Bart, you reeked of booze and there was a bottle of Crown Royal scattered all over the cab."

"Oh, for Christ sake."

Doc interceded. "Bart," he said, "what's the last thing you remember?"

I lay there for a moment trying to shake the image Fred had painted of the accident. "I went to see Benny out at Lasko, he was working on the police boat." I felt a drop of sweat trickle slowly down my temple. "Then I went to Pebble Beach."

"Why?" Fred asked.

"Because of the pebbles I found in the bottom of the boat."

"What boat?" Fred asked, looking puzzled.

"The one I found in the marsh."

"You found a boat?"

"Yeah. Ask Benny Langthorne, he knows."

"We'll check it out. So, you went to Pebble Beach because of these pebbles. What did you do there?"

"Well... I talked to some people at a cottage. I think the name was Riskowsky."

Fred wrote it down.

"They told me the boat might belong to somebody around there." I remembered going over to Riley's Rest to do a little snooping around after that, but I wasn't sure I wanted to admit this to the police right then and besides it was all pretty fuzzy. I inhaled deeply. "That's the last thing I remember." I didn't have to fake being worn out, but I closed my eyes and moaned weakly just the same.

Doc picked right up on it. "Maybe you should come back later, Fred. He needs some rest now."

"Okay," Fred said. "Bart, we'll talk some more later."

I grunted, but kept my eyes closed.

"How's the pain, Bart? Let's help you out a little." Doc stuck a syringe into my IV tube and within a few minutes I was again dead to the world.

"Jesus! You look like hell," Nick Taylor said when I opened my eyes a few hours later. He was sitting in a chair at the end of my bed with the newspaper open in his lap.

"Thanks, I needed to hear that." I closed my eyes and felt somebody wrap me on the head with that hammer again. When the pounding stopped, I gestured to his paper and asked, "What's the latest?"

"Well, you know, gas prices up, grain prices down, farmers complaining. Same old shit."

I couldn't help but smile to myself. This was Nick Taylor trying to cheer me up.

"But seriously, man," he said, "you look pretty rough." He examined my face as though I weren't there. "Worse than when old Roman sent you head over heels into the crossbar that time in Meath Park."

"Maybe I should have a look."

"I wouldn't if I were you," he said.

"There's a hand mirror over by the sink," I said. Nick handed it to me. He wasn't exaggerating. Both my eyes were black, nearly swollen shut and there were cuts and scrapes on my face. A mummy-like wrapping covered most of my skull. My body felt like it had been through a thrashing machine. There was a particularly nasty feel to my left knee, my hockey knee.

"You were right," I took a deep breath that made me keenly aware of a stabbing pain in my ribs, "I shouldn't have."

"So what the hell happened?" Nick said.

I thought it over. "I don't know, I just can't seem to remem…" A flash of memory burned through the fog. But what? A woody, dusty smell, the dank light from a smudged window. Something in the closet. A label attached to a suitcase. Something deep red on the shelf. My concentration was interrupted when I heard footsteps down the hall.

In came Rosie, a bunch of flowers in her hand, then Stuart, carrying a wicker picnic basket and an arm full of books and magazines.

"Nice flowers," Nick said, standing up to make room. Rosie put the bouquet on the bedside table, while Stuart placed the basket on the stand at the foot of the bed.

I'm not sure why, but the sight of Annie walking in a minute later turned me to mush. I felt tears streaming down my swollen cheeks. Guess she made me realize just how glad I was to be alive. My daughter's face was filled with apprehension as she came over and took my hand. "Hi," she said, her voice shaky, "how are you?" She examined my face with tender eyes.

"I'm fine, sweetheart," I sniffed. "I'm a tough old bugger, eh."

"Yeah, I know." She tried to smile.

"How's the old Toyota running?" I said.

"Oh, Daddy." Her smile widened.

While Annie stood holding my hands, Rosie placed a full dinner setting in front of me with cutlery from the silver chest and even a linen napkin that she'd shaped into a swan. On the china plate was a breast of roast chicken, *sans* skin, I noticed, oven roasted potatoes and a nice salad. Old Mr. Sawchuk, my roommate, couldn't help but drool at the sight, especially when the white-clad orderly rolled in with his supper that resembled dog chow with a few wilted leaves on the side; meatloaf and garden salad, he was told.

Two days later I was discharged, having been in the hospital longer than was necessary in my opinion. Doc had removed the mummy wrapping, put a tensor bandage on my knee, given me a prescription for pain, and cautioned me that blows to the head could take unpredictable turns. Rosie helped me gather up my few possessions and took a stack of magazines to the waiting room. Mr. Sawchuk looked a little hungry as I said goodbye.

I was glad to be home, but felt rotten. I took a pain killer and dozed off for a couple of hours.

At noon Stuart huffed in, out of breath, and flopped into his chair at the kitchen table. "Sure glad you're home, Dad," he said.

"Yeah, me too," I said. "Did you run all the way from school?"

"Yeah, I'm in training." Stuart was always in training for something.

"How's school going?"

He made a face before saying, "Mr. Chilliak gave us another class on drinking and driving. That's the third one this week."

Rosie looked over, a pinched look on her face. "Stuart, please go wash your hands."

"When's Randall getting here?" Stuart asked.

"He'll be here in time for supper. You don't even ask about your sister?" Rosie ruffled his hair briskly. "Now go and wash those hands."

"Do you see what's going on?" she whispered sharply. "Everybody thinks you had an accident because you were drunk."

"Well, that's just too damn bad," I said.

"You've got to tell people."

"Why," I said, "so Mr. Chilliak can quit giving drinking and driving lessons?"

Rosie gave up and began serving dinner. My eyes were bigger than my stomach, and I left a good portion of my meal on the plate. My usual forty-five minute nap turned into a couple of hours. I awoke to the racket that only two women can make chattering in the kitchen. It was Rosie and her sister.

"He's not going to, is he?" Myra said. "He can't be that stupid." Myra is an outspoken lady who can't help but express her opinion on things. Knowing something about those things, however, is not essential.

"Hello, Myra," I said making my way stiffly down the steep loft steps.

"How are you?" she asked, narrowing her eyes in the way people do when they don't really want to hear about it. "Your face looks like hell."

"Thanks," I said, groaning a bit on the last couple of steps.

"So," Myra said, "it sounds like you stuck your nose in where it don't belong."

I gave Rosie a questioning look. "Yes," she said with justified firmness, "I told her."

Myra gave me her *I'm one up on you* smirk.

"Bart, you know I want you to keep out of it," Rosie said.

"Rosie," I protested, "I didn't get into it. I merely stumbled on a boat out at Lasko Beach."

"And you nearly got yourself killed for your trouble."

I didn't want to throw any more wood on the fire, so I kept my mouth shut, but Rosie fanned the flames. "Are you going to pursue this?"

"I don't know what you're talking about."

"There's no good reason for you to get involved."

"Now that you mention it," I said sinking into my chair at the head of the table, "there is a good reason."

"Yes?" Rosie said.

"My friend, Nick Taylor."

She rolled her blue eyes skyward.

"It's about loyalty?" I said.

"Loyalty," Rosie scoffed, tossing the dishcloth into the sink.

"Yeah, I don't have to remind you."

"None of my loyalties are going to get me killed," she said.

"And my helping Nick isn't going to get…"

"Don't be such an idiot," she shot back. "Look what happened already."

Myra looked at me with disgust, but knew better than to butt in when Rosie was steamrolling.

Rosie continued. "Is there some reason you think Bart Bartowski can do a better job than the RCMP and detectives from the city?"

"I don't know," I said, "but one thing I do know, I care what happens to Nick. The police don't. They've got their man. All they want to do is put more nails in his coffin."

Rosie sighed. "At least do this for me. If you learn something that might help Nick, give it to his lawyer. That's his bloody job after all."

"I will. Trust me, I have no intention of going through this again." I gingerly touched my bruised face.

"Well, I just want you to remember that you've got a wife and a family. And as far as I'm concerned, we deserve your loyalty, certainly as much as Nick Taylor."

My head started pounding.

"You don't look so good," Myra said.

"I don't feel so good," I said weakly.

"Don't you see?" Rosie said. Her face squeezed in on itself and her eyes welled up with tears.

I got up with some difficulty and went to where she stood leaning against the counter. "Rosie," I put my arms around her and stroked her back gently. "I'm not going to do anything that would hurt you or Stu or Annie. I want you to believe that."

Rosie dabbed at her nose with a tissue. Her voice cracked a little as she said, "I do." All the coolness was gone for that instant.

I remembered when we were teenagers, Rosie and I, in the forty-nine Plymouth that Uncle Rudy had given me after he couldn't drive anymore. We would sit in that musty old car for hours, just talking. Rosie was a shy thing back then, demanding nothing except to be included in my life. She'd had a pretty hard upbringing. One of eight kids, a working mother and a father who wasn't around most of the time, she didn't get much attention in that household. I guess that's why she didn't demand a lot from me. And, of course, at sixteen, I was pretty self-centered, so it worked out quite well. But now Rosie was everything to me, my lover, my partner, my support system, and for this moment, at least, my friend.

Myra set the teapot and some cups on the table along with a plate of oatmeal-coconut cookies that Rosie had baked earlier. A few minutes later Rosie returned from the bathroom, face washed, hair combed, but still a little red around the eyes. She gave me one of her little shy smiles, lasting only a moment, but conveying that the worst has passed.

"So, did you hear the latest?" Myra put in, shifting her ample posterior on the kitchen chair. "The police have been grilling those poor Taylor kids. Helen Mousie down at the Co-op told me about it. You know, as far as I'm concerned, they shouldn't be allowed to question those kids at all, and I bet there was no lawyer there either. I mean those bloody police," Myra pulled briskly on the collar of her plaid, wool shirt, "who do they think they are?"

"Imagine what those poor kids must be going through," Rosie said. "I wonder if they're getting any help?"

"'They certainly should be," Myra said, "after all, those school counselors are paid to do more than just shuffle paper, eh."

"And those children are completely innocent," Rosie said.

"So is Nick," I said.

"You have no doubts about that?" Myra asked in a dubious tone. But before I could answer, she snorted, "Well, you never can tell, can you? Jealousy can make people do things, eh. Who knows in those circumstances? Can anybody say how they'd react?"

"If they didn't get into those circumstances in the first place," Rosie said, "they wouldn't have to react."

"Well, you know that Wilma," Myra scoffed, "she's always flaunted herself in front of the men."

"Oh come on," I protested.

"Well, she has," Myra said.

"Just because she isn't some cow who hasn't the will or the way to look half way decent doesn't make her a tramp," I said. Myra eyed me frigidly. "Why shouldn't she take advantage of her God given attributes?" I immediately knew I was on thin ice when I noticed Rosie's eyes narrow, but I forged ahead just the same. "Why shouldn't a woman dress nice and look as attractive as she can?"

Rosie and Myra remained silent, just staring at me. I looked from one to the other. "What?" I said. Rosie just rolled her eyes, and Myra, who hadn't had a man in her life for years, reached for another cookie.

Thankfully, the doorbell rang just then so I was spared any rebuttal. Rosie ushered in Fred Snell. He was in uniform today.

Fred declined a cup of tea, but did accept one of Rosie's oatmeal-coconut cookies. Myra gave Corporal Snell the cold shoulder on behalf of the Taylor kids, I guess. I invited Fred out to the garden where we would be out of earshot of my dear wife and her sister.

"We talked to the Riskowsky girl," Fred started. "She told us that when you left, you were headed over to Rileys."

I sat down on the edge of the raised bed where I'd planted leaf lettuce and white radishes.

"So?" Fred asked.

I didn't want to admit to break and enter. "That's where my memory just kind of craps out," I said.

"You mean you still can't remember?" Fred's face said he wasn't buying it. "You must remember something?"

"Well?"

"Think back," he said, "you walked over to Riley's cabin. Did you walk along the water or take the lane?"

"I took the lane."

"Did you knock on the door?"

"Yeah, I guess I knocked."

"And?"

"There was no answer."

"Did you go inside?" Fred asked, his voice rising in pitch.

"Yeah," I said, "I guess I did. But the door wasn't locked."

"So, did you see anything unusual?"

"Not that I can recall."

"Do you remember what happened?"

I made a face. "Not really."

Fred's voice rose even higher. "What do you think happened?"

"I don't know, but something must have happened."

"So you have no recollection of how you got to Ireland's?"

"None," I said.

Fred raised his eyebrows in exasperation.

I picked up the hoe and pawed at the ground with it. "So, what did you find out?" I asked.

"Not much. The Rileys are away in Europe visiting their daughter. There are very few people staying at the lake right now. We did talk to one neighbour, he thinks they're planning to sell the place."

"What about the boat?"

"Yeah, we're pretty sure it came from there. Bart, I gotta tell you, Hutt doesn't like your story. So if anything comes to mind, anything at all, I want to know about it."

"Did you check the boathouse?"

"Yeah, nothing in there, but it looks like it may have been used recently."

My knee was throbbing and my head felt not much better. "Sorry Fred, I've got an appointment with Doc at three, but before I go, I wanted to ask you something. There's a rumour going around that you've been grilling Nick's kids. Is that true?"

"We talked to them."

"Is that fair? I mean really, they're just kids and they've been through a lot." I used the hoe to hoist myself up. "I think that's pretty shabby, Fred."

7

The smell of roast beef and gravy filled the house. The table was set and there was a bouquet of fresh flowers at the centre. The bottle of wine I'd been ordered to bring home sat on the counter, breathing. I think Rosie wanted to impress Randall. Annie came into the kitchen and gave me a hug. I only winced a little as she lovingly squeezed my bruised ribs.

Randall descended from the loft where he and Stuart had been messing around with the computer. Randall stuck his hand out and said, "Real sorry to hear about your accident, Mr. Bartowski."

"It wasn't an accident," I protested.

"What was it then, Daddy?" Annie asked.

"I don't want to talk about it right now," I said.

She examined my face with a critical eye. "How are you feeling?"

"Ah, hell, I'm fine. How about some wine? Lori down at the liquor store said this Okanagan red would be good. Rosie, where are the glasses?"

Randall accepted a glass, but Annie declined. Rosie put some puff-pastry hors-d'oeuvres on the coffee table in the living room. We seldom ate in there, but in deference to Annie's visit and company, Rosie broke that rule. Of course Stuart, smelling the pastries, pulled himself away from the computer to partake and though crumbs scattered over the new couch as he ate, neither Rosie nor I complained.

Randall was very attentive to Annie, but her response seemed less than reciprocal this evening. Their usual touchy feely behavior, which I normally dislike, was missing and ironically that bothered me.

Randall was polite, considerate and most importantly, he genuinely liked our Annie. The first we'd heard of him was when Annie came home one weekend and all she could talk about was this boy she'd met and how helpful he was, him being ahead of her in the environmental studies program. I think she also mentioned his curly hair and cute butt. Then about a month later she brought him home. That was almost a year ago.

I refilled our glasses as Randall enthusiastically discussed his master's thesis and described what he hoped to accomplish in his work-study program that summer at Stuart Lake. His area of interest was wildlife, their numbers and migration patterns. I had consented to the arrangement when he'd agreed to assess the environmental impact that mining would have on the wildlife of Stuart Lake and surrounding areas, though I didn't have much faith that his findings would cut any ice with the government.

After digging into the prime rib with Yorkshire pudding that Rosie had laid on, Randall and I went down to my office—the bear pit Rosie calls it—to discuss his work at the lodge. On my wall map, I pointed out Stuart Lake and the area that Capex International had staked out. "The lodge sits at the end of a deep bay next to a long, tumbling rapids," I said. "Some big fish have been caught off those rocks." I proudly showed him pictures on the wall of thirty and forty pounders. "From the lodge you can watch a family of bald eagles that come back every year to a small island that floats a few hundred yards out."

We talked more about his research; he told me he would observe wildlife in a grid pattern to see what activity occurred in each area. It seemed logical. "How much time will it take?" I asked.

"The most useful data would come over a year of observations," he said, "but three seasons is adequate.

Did that mean he would be staying for three seasons, I wondered? After about an hour of this, there was a light knock at the door.

Annie poked her head in and said, "How're you guys doing down here? It's awful quiet."

"Your Dad's been filling me in," Randall said. "The place looks awesome."

"Dad, can I drag him away," Annie said, "I want to go for a walk before it gets dark."

"Sure honey, we're pretty much finished here."

"I'm coming up to the lodge too, by the way," Annie said.

"Great," I said, "now I won't have to do dishes."

"Well, I wouldn't go that far, Dad, and besides," she said teasingly, "I may be busy in the evenings." She put her arm around Randall's waist. I was glad to see that for some reason.

"But Randall may be busy too," I said, "swabbing out boats, chopping wood and hauling out the, you know what."

"Daddy." She was giggling as they climbed the stairs.

Stuart insisted that they accompany him over to cadets in the Catholic Church basement as part of their walk. Annie protested, but Randall agreed, so the three of them headed out together.

"He's such a nice boy," Rosie said after they'd closed the door behind them. "He treats Annie so well. And Stuart."

"I just hope he doesn't get under foot up at the lodge," I said.

"Oh, why would he? And besides, he'll be doing something for us, and for the environment," she added.

"I do something for the environment every day." Rosie gave me that *here we go again* expression, but I couldn't help myself. "We have the catch and release program. We fly out the garbage, at no little expense I need not remind you. We respect that wilderness, Rosie, and you know it. Have done for nearly fifteen years, and it's better for it."

"But there are new developments at the university."

"There are more fish in those lakes now than when we first went up there. That's good enough for me."

"I don't disagree, honey, but it can't hurt to have another point of view. And maybe," Rosie's face hardened," he'll be able to help us fight off those Capex buggers."

The Taylors had an older home, a barn-shaped two-story. The colour scheme—purple with pink trim—was Wilma's choice and though Nick complained bitterly, Wilma stood firm. Fortunately a giant carragana hedge hid the house from the street.

Across the tracks, looming high over their home was a hulking hundred-foot monster that was close to extinction. From its mouth, billions of bushels of grain had been disgorged and sent westward by rail, then shipped throughout the world. The now defunct elevator had been run by the Saskatchewan Wheat Pool, a group of farmers who had got together to gain some control over the collection and transportation of their product to market.

Since railway abandonment had begun in the seventies, multinationals had inexorably taken over, building giant inland terminals and transporting grain by truck. The subject of deteriorating highways ranks second only to the weather for what passes as chitchat on the prairies.

The huge orange structure behind the Taylor's house sat idle. It, along with hundreds just like it waited to be dealt with. Some had been imploded, the odd one moved and others dismantled. Some were less than fifteen or twenty years old, with generations of life left in them. A fellow from Crystal Creek, some sort of artist, had a plan to turn one into a theatre. Live theatre. "A real prairie experience," he told some of us at coffee row one day. "Enjoy a fowl supper on the truck deck, before being elevated to the uppermost reaches for a good prairie story, with prairie actors and writers, maybe a hockey story in honour of the greats like Gordie Howe, or a story of the Riel Rebellion that took place not twenty miles from here." He figured people would come from all over to see that. But while it waited, the only thing the elevator was good for was stopping the cold northeast wind from finding its way through the cracks and crannies of the Taylor's old house.

"Hi you guys," Wilma said, looking a little the worse for wear. "Come on in."

"Don't tell me you walked?" Nick said, coming out of the living room wearing comfortable, woolly slippers and carrying a beer. "I didn't hear no car."

"Yes, Nick," I said, "we walked. Just because you guys drive three blocks to church doesn't mean everybody's foot challenged."

"Hey, we gotta drive, otherwise how'd we carry all that loot for the offering."

"All right, all right," Wilma said, "come in and sit down." Her voice faltered a little. "It's good to see you guys," she said, dabbing at her eyes furtively. "How're you, Bart, okay?"

"Oh yeah," I winced, "I'm fine."

"He can take a shit kicking," Nick said. "Hell, I've seen him play a whole period of hockey with a concussion. He didn't even know he had it."

"He's not eighteen anymore," Rosie said.

"How about a beer?" Nick offered.

"I'll have one," I said.

"Rosie?"

"You got some tea, Wilma?" she asked.

"I'll put on the kettle," Wilma said.

Settled in the living room, their golden lab, Chipshot, sitting amiably on my feet, I said, "I thought it was kind of a lousy thing, the police questioning Jake and Susan like that. Can't they think of anything else to do besides harass your kids. I let Snell have it too when he came over to the house this afternoon."

"You got it wrong, Bart," Nick said.

"Yeah," Wilma said, "they asked to talk to the police. Susan had the idea that if they could just tell those detectives what a great dad Nick is, they would see that he couldn't have done this horrible thing."

"Damn kids," Nick said, affectionately, "they even dressed up to make a good impression."

"I guess I really put my foot in it with Fred, then." I should have known Myra was talking through her hat.

"Don't worry about Fred," Nick said, "but that goddamned Klassen outright asked Jake if he thinks I killed Harvey Kristoff? Can you bloody well believe that?"

Nick handed me a bottle of beer while Wilma brought in a tray with a teapot and cups and saucers. She poured tea for her and Rosie while Nick and I sipped on our *Pils* and dipped into a bowl of mixed nuts.

"Have you seen that new greens keeper," Nick said, "the fat fuck?"

"Nick," Wilma scolded.

"Yeah, I met him," I said.

"The guy must weigh a ton."

"He's not a bad guy," I said.

"And his weight isn't necessarily his fault," Rosie said. "Maybe he's got a glandular problem."

"Yeah," Nick groaned, "his stomach."

"He likes what you did at the course."

"What's not to like?"

"It's a good course," I conceded.

"And Nick made it that way," Wilma said. "He worked hard, too. How many nights he didn't get home 'till midnight? How many times he worked on his day off? That park board never once made him feel appreciated. And then that…oh, that damn Harvey," she spat.

"Well, fucking him didn't help," Nick threw in casually, then chugged on his beer. Rosie and I stared at the carpet, a nice brown one with little squiggly things running through it.

"I didn't…fuck him," Wilma said.

But Nick was having none of it. "Bullshit," he said.

"I didn't," Wilma said, "I just wanted…"

"What? His money? His house? Or just his big dick?"

"Stop it, stop it," Wilma shouted. "You don't understand."

"Okay, so tell me something that I can understand. This ought be good," he said to Rosie and I who were still examining the carpet.

"I just thought I could help. I could convince him to lay off you."

"How?"

"Just by…I don't know, being friendly."

"Friendly," Nick said disgustedly.

"Yes." Wilma sat rigid, her eyes streaming tears.

"What the hell's wrong with you?" Nick said.

The tears carried rivulets of mascara down her cheeks. "How can you talk this way in front of our friends?"

"What way?" Nick said.

"Oh, you're so righteous, aren't you?" Wilma said. "You've never done anything wrong."

"I never fucked nobody," Nick shouted angrily, and rapped his empty beer bottle on the tabletop.

No one said a word for a dog's breath. In fact Chipshot took the opportunity to get up off my now sleeping feet and head into the kitchen where we heard his long tongue lapping at the water dish.

Jake bustled in. "How come it's so quiet in here?"

When nobody else responded, I said, "We better be going, right honey?"

Rosie got up off the couch. "Wilma, call tomorrow." We knew what they'd be discussing.

A half-moon loomed over the shoulder of the Pool elevator as we walked down the darkening street toward home. Neither Rosie nor I commented on Nick and Wilma's exchange. We could well imagine the cutting conversations that had passed between the two.

"God, that must be hard to live with," Rosie finally said as we approached our house on Canuck Crescent. It would be surrounded by flowering Canola in a couple of months and my allergies would kick in big time.

"She says she didn't screw Harvey." I said.

"Yeah?" Rosie sounded skeptical.

I hunched my shoulders. "Well, it comes down to her word against that of some anonymous tip, now that Harvey's gone." Cutting a swath between the fields of Canola was the abandoned railway track. Only a few trains ran through the province these days, yet rail still criss-crossed the land, probably too expensive to uproot.

"I feel sorry for those poor children," she said. "Stuart said the kids at school are making jokes."

"You can't blame them," I said, "after all, this thing *is* like a bloody soap opera."

"Even so," Rosie said, opening the front door. We stepped through the threshold and found ourselves crunching broken glass under our feet.

"What the hell? I told Stuart not to slam the damn door."

"Look," Rosie pointed at a rock that sat a few feet inside the porch.

8

Rosie's face went pale. "Call the police, Bart."

"Now Rosie, don't go getting crazy. We don't know what happened here and besides what are they going to do, take finger prints off this rock?"

"I don't know, maybe. But..." Her lips trembled.

"All right, all right. I'll call in the morning."

"No, now. What if Stuart and Annie had been home? What if the buggers throw more rocks, or worse?"

Constable Stan Renwick who was a regular on the night watch arrived within a half hour of my phone call. "Could have been just a prank," Renwick ventured. "Someone fooling around. Maybe a kid."

But even as he said these words, I rejected them. I wondered if it could be a message from the same person who had pushed me into Ireland's Ravine.

"It's kind of unusual," Renwick said, holding up the rock contained in a clear, plastic evidence bag.

"It looks to me like it came from Pebble Beach," I said.

"How can you tell?" Renwick asked.

"By the pinkish hue and the shiny surface," I said.

"That shiny surface might help us get some finger prints, but I wouldn't count on it," Renwick said, as he started for the door. "We'll ask around in the morning, see if anyone saw anything."

After he left, I joined Rosie and Stuart at the kitchen table. Stu, still wearing his cadet uniform, was fidgeting and Rosie held two rumpled tissues in her hand, though her eyes were cold and dry. Randall and Annie leaned against the counter, heads down, arms folded.

"Well?" Rosie said.

"Well," I repeated, "it was like I said. There isn't much they can do."

"I bet it was the Jenkins kid," Stu said. "He's always throwing stuff."

"Maybe," I said.

"He's never broken any windows before." Rosie said.

"Well, who then?" Stuart asked, his legs bouncing up and down as though they were spring loaded.

Rosie looked worried.

"How was cadets?" I asked Stuart, trying to get off the topic of the rock.

"I was officer in charge again, since Captain Jarvis wasn't there. Again. He was probably drunk."

"Stu," Rosie said.

"Well, he always smells like booze."

Rosie and I exchanged grimaces.

"So what did the officer in charge do?" I asked.

"I led some drills," Stuart said, "then we planned the Canada Day parade."

"Was Jake there?" Rosie asked.

"No. You know, 'cause of his dad. And his mom. I wouldn't go either," he added. "Dad? If you want, I can stay up and guard the house."

"That won't be necessary son, but thanks for the offer."

Rosie gave him a hug around the neck. "Okay," he broke her strangle hold and headed for his room, "I'm goin' to bed. G'night."

After he'd headed down the hall to his bedroom, Annie said, "Dad, nobody's ever thrown a rock at our house before. Ever." She eyed me gravely. "And look at you."

I thought I'd been healing quite well.

"I'm scared, Dad."

It felt awful to hear my daughter say that she was afraid in her own home, the home I was supposed to keep secure. And I didn't want to admit it to her, but I was scared too.

Fred Snell's inquiries the next morning in the crescent revealed nothing. No one in the neighborhood had seen or heard anything, nor were there any fingerprints on the rock. Fred repeated the admonition, declared so strikingly by the rock: "Stay out of it."

However, despite the rock or maybe because of it, I had a real hankering to return to Riley's Rest. I needed to be in that bedroom again, look into that closet again.

After a breakfast of egg-on-toast with three cups of coffee, I jumped into Rosie's van and took the back road out to Pebble Beach. I drove by Rileys slowly, did a u-turn, and like before nestled into the willows alongside the gravel lane. Since Juliette's MG was parked in Riskowsky's driveway I thought I'd stop in and say hello. Rounding the corner that led to the deck, I saw long hair crowning a female form. But when I said a hearty, "Good morning," I was confronted not by the welcoming face of Juliette, but by a much older woman, replete with wrinkles, graying hair, and an unpleasant scowl.

She was perhaps the mother, if not the grandmother. An overflowing ashtray and a cup of black coffee sat on a TV table next to her. She was thin and her pallor was sallow, matching the faded, yellow housedress she wore.

"My name is Bart Bartowski," I said. She frowned at me. "I was here about a week ago and I met your daughter, Juliette."

"Yeah," she said, looking faintly interested. "And by the way, she ain't my daughter."

"Excuse me, I'm terribly sorry, I just assumed. In any case, it was with regard to the Riley's place."

She looked at me dubiously. "Just a minute," she said. "Fred," she shouted, still looking straight at me, then even louder, "Fred, get out here."

"What the hell are you yellin' about?" he said, kicking the screen door open with a bare foot. "Oh, hello," he said when he saw me, "didn't know anyone else was out here." He must have weighed at least two fifty and was only about five foot eight or nine. His belly would have hung well below his belt had he been wearing one, but he wore a swimsuit. Speedo. He held a towel at his side that wouldn't have dried his thinning hair, let alone his rotund body.

"My name's Bart Bartowski," I said, "I was just saying to your wife..."

"She ain't my wife," he said, "she's my sister."

"Oh, I beg your pardon." It definitely wasn't my day. "As I was saying to your sister," I carried on, "I was here about a week ago and I met Juliette."

"You're a little old for her, aren't ya?" he interrupted.

"No. It's not like that," I said, feeling blood rush to my face. "She just gave me some information." I was beginning to wonder if this was worth it. "Would you folks know anything about the Rileys?"

"Haven't seen those Rileys in a coon's age," his sister said, picking tobacco from between her front teeth. I couldn't believe Juliette was related to these hillbillies.

Fred set a suspicious eye on me. "Why are you interested in the Rileys?"

"Well, it actually has to do with their boat. A twelve foot aluminum with a motor…that, uh, gives off a lot of smoke," which coincidentally I was doing at the moment, "and I, that is we of the regional park board…"

"I'll tell you what, son," he said, interrupting my blarney and setting his behind gingerly into a white resin deck chair, "we haven't seen hide nor hair of anyone over there since the police came poking around. You ain't from the police are you?"

"Oh, no. I really didn't mean to disturb you folks," I said, "I'll be gettin' outta your hair now." That hillbilly jargon was contagious.

"Hold on, young fella, why don't you stick around and have a beer?" He ignored the return of his sister's scowl. "It's kinda lonely out here. Not many people around this early in the season."

I could imagine he needed someone other than his sister to talk to.

"That's generous of you, but I've got a lot of work to do, and I better get to it." Just for good measure, I added, "You all have a good day now."

As I turned down the road toward Riley's Rest, I heard a dog yelp behind me. I turned and saw Juliette.

She was walking a dusty little poodle on a leash. The dog began yapping.

"What are you doing here?" she said, squatting to quiet the poodle.

"Oh, just some more poking around," I said, quoting her Uncle Fred.

"How are you feeling?" she said, examining my face.

"I'll survive," I said stoically, not wanting to invite sympathy.

"The police said you were drinking and had an accident."

"Is that what they said?"

"That was the gist." I could see she was disappointed.

I felt embarrassed, but at the same time I didn't feel like defending myself. "I wasn't entirely honest with you when I came by before."

"Yeah, I know, you were here about that murder." The poodle jumped up on her knee and tried to lick her face. "Down, Lilly," she said, stroking the dog's curly head.

"I'm still trying to find out who might have been driving Riley's boat that day."

"Why?"

"Because it just might have been the murderer."

"Oh." Her dark eyes widened.

"I'd like to go back over there." I nodded toward Rileys.

"What for?" she said.

"I don't know, maybe it'll help jog my memory."

"I'll go with you."

"No you won't," I said.

"I know where the key is," she said, tilting her head and looking at me through her long lashes.

"Okay, but you stay outside, agreed?"

"Whatever you say."

Right. We continued along the lane and down Riley's drive, Lilly leading the way. Nothing had changed much since the last time I'd been there. Uncut grass, empty driveway, blinds closed.

"Do you know the Rileys well?" I asked.

"Not really, we kind of look out for each other's places. That's how I know where the key is."

We approached the door that had been unlocked on my earlier visit. This time it was locked. Handing me the dog leash, Juliette went over to the railing of the deck, got up on her tiptoes and reached under the low hanging eve, her skin momentarily visible above the nicely shaped Calvin Klein's. She located the key and handed it to me with a satisfied grin.

The key, a little rusty from winters under the eve, grated in the lock. The first thing I recognized as I opened the door was the chrome kitchen table that now occupied the centre of the room. A couple of empty beer cans sat on the windowsill as though the owners' last act of the season had been to toast the lake, before leaving for the winter.

"Looks like no one's been here for a while," Juliette said. "See the cobwebs?" She pointed to the doorway of the bedroom where a cluster of cobwebs stretched from the upper to the side frame. I tentatively turned the door handle, and maybe as a show of bravery, threw the bedroom door open in one motion. Pushing the cobwebs aside, I proceeded slowly into the room.

"I opened the curtains," I said almost to myself, "and I looked into the closet..." In the closet was a suitcase. A good suitcase with a leather I.D. tag attached to it.

The word ARM tooled into it. As I looked to the upper shelf the image's became even more vivid. A red wig, a scarf. I could have picked them up, they were now so clearly drawn in my memory. The wig, a deep auburn, thick and synthetic. The scarf, translucent, but still rich with orange colour.

"I remember now," I said.

"You do?" Juliette looked a little apprehensive.

"Yes." I flattened the bedroom door against the wall. "There was probably somebody hiding behind this door." And whoever it was must have knocked me out. But how did I end up at Ireland's Ravine? And why? I felt a sudden chill. "Let's get out of here."

I headed for the door just as Juliette did. Wedged into the narrow doorway, we came together, face-to-face, thigh-to-thigh, chest to... well you get the idea.

"You remember Josh," she breathed, "he was so immature, and possessive. You know the time you came over? He went ballistic after you left. Said I couldn't ever wear a bikini again. Unbelievable, don't you think?"

Yeah, unbelievable.

I felt her hands on my waist and I was rendered speechless when she pressed her hips against mine. "I need a more mature man," she said.

I couldn't move. She wouldn't move. Did she have a hold of my belt loops? Did her lips pucker? Did her eyes begin to close?

"What was that?" I said.

"What was what?"

"That sound." All was quiet except for Lilly dragging her leash along the kitchen floor.

"Don't worry," she said, "there's nobody around."

"Yeah, you're probably right." But by then we were in the kitchen and out of the danger zone.

After leaving Juliette with her aunt and uncle, I headed for Ireland's Ravine. I needed to see the place where I had allegedly rolled my truck. I took the shortcut past Grayham Point where the late Harvey Kristoff had lived with his wife, Ellen. I wondered how she was doing, and made a mental note to visit her sometime in the near future.

I turned the corner and drove the couple of klicks to Ireland's Ravine. Tire tracks were faint, but still visible on the shoulder where my truck had gone over. Skid marks slashed through the grass and bushes below. The rolling truck had ripped up the ground, torn out small trees and flattened the area where it had come to rest. I felt a sickening gush of anxiety course through my body, almost as if it recalled what my mind could not.

I slowly and carefully made my way down the steep slope to the bottom of the embankment. Something glinted in the sunlight. I pushed aside some fireweed and picked up the square mirror that had previously graced the driver's side door. I knew it was the driver's side, because last fall I had knocked off the other one backing into the garage. Stuart had given me no end of grief about that one.

Struggling back to the road, it struck me that where skidding and sliding had naturally occurred on the slope, no such marks appeared on the shoulder of the road. The faintly visible treads suggested that the truck had purposefully rolled off the road and into the ditch. The presence of a smashed bottle of whiskey and spilled liquor in my cab was apparently evidence enough for the police to forego a critical examination of the scene. Just another drunk driver.

Returning empty-handed from the post office the following day, I found Rosie sitting at the kitchen table, a cup of coffee in front of her.

"There was a phone call for you," she said.

"Who was it?"

"I don't know. Some woman."

"What did she want?"

Rosie raised her eyebrows. "Didn't say, just wanted to talk to Bart and said to call her back. Left her number."

"Where is it?" I looked toward the telephone stand.

"Bart, what's going on?"

"What do you mean?"

"Who's this woman, won't even leave her name?"

"How should I know?"

"Are you back at this thing?"

"Rosie, I was out at Ireland's and I'm sure my truck was pushed over that embankment deliberately."

"And how does that help Nick?"

"I don't know, but it sure looks like someone doesn't want me snooping around."

"You better damn well listen to them too."

I picked up the phone and dialed.

"Hello, this is Bart Bartowski."

"It's me," Juliette said.

"Oh hello," I said as formally as I could.

"I just saw someone at Rileys."

"Who?"

"Come out to the cottage."

"Is that necessary?"

"If you want to know who it was," she said.

"Okay, I guess I could do that."

"So," Rosie said after I hung up, "who was it?"

"The Riskowsky girl at Pebble Beach. She's got something out there she wants me to see."

"I'll just bet she does."

"Rosie," I pleaded." Rosie has always been a little possessive. Some of that can be chalked up to adolescent jealousy, like when Darlene Yancew moved to town with her parents who had bought the drugstore. She was sixteen at the time, and pretty in a promising sort of way. Feeling a little sorry for her, I decided it was my duty, if not to befriend her, at least to make her feel welcome. Rosie was keenly aware of my attention to her and let me know it. That was my first taste of Rosie's wrath. But I don't think either of us was quite ready for the full-grown Juliette Riskowsky.

I spotted Juliette standing in the sunlit yard. She'd obviously been waiting for me. I couldn't help but notice the black shorts she wore. I guess they would be described as short shorts as they displayed the entire length of her tanned legs. Above that she had on one of those abbreviated T-shirts.

"Hello, Bart." She waved as I got out of Rosie's mini-van, which all of a sudden felt stodgy and very un-cool. I should have been hopping out of a sporty convertible like the rest of the mid-life crisis victims, wearing rugs and chasing kids half their age.

"Hello," I said, sucking in my stomach, ignoring my sore knee and walking jauntily over to Juliette whose stillness I found disconcerting. Her hair, thick and shiny, cascaded over her strong shoulders. Her tanned belly was flat and its bareness somehow expressed an invitation to explore both nether and yon. My eyes involuntarily went to both places.

"There was someone at Rileys," she said.

My explorations ceased.

"I didn't actually see the person. I was coming back from walking Lilly and I noticed a truck parked out front."

"What kind of truck?"

"An old one. It was green and pretty rusted out. There was no tail gate. Just as I snuck behind the bushes to see who it was, it took off."

"Dammit, Juliette," I said, angry that she would put herself in harm's way. But I did appreciate her attention to detail, because now I had a good idea what ARM stood for.

"Bart, would you like to come in for a minute?"

The truck, the letter of application and the initials A.R.M. It all came together.

"My aunt and uncle are gone."

What about the wig?

"We have the place to ourselves," she said, "we could…"

"What?" I said.

In response, she slid her hand across her smooth belly and up under her T-shirt. "Come in," she said. The moment was terrifyingly intimate, as though nothing else existed except the warm spring morning, her body, and the effect she surely knew she was having on me.

Me? Thirty-nine plus, not in great shape, bad knees, covered in cuts and contusions, and she wanted me? She could pick and choose; have any man she desired. Well, at least my hair was mostly all there, and I had a manly moustache. But, nonetheless, I gave her my meaningful look, and more reluctantly than you can possibly imagine, said, "Probably not a good idea."

She met my gaze, challenging me.

"I really have to go," I said hoarsely. "I gotta find that truck."

Disappointment showed on her face, but she recovered quickly. "I'll go with you."

Not a bad compromise I thought, relieved, yet a little dissatisfied. "Okay, but once we get there, you'll stay out of the way. Agreed?"

"Agreed," she said with a tilt of her head that suggested she'd do as she pleased, nor would I object.

Climbing into the none-too-tidy minivan, we drove the lane that skirted the lake. Arriving the back way, I thought, would attract less attention at White Pine, where I was convinced I would find the owner of a rusty, green pickup and the initials A.R.M. The breeze coming through the open window blew Juliette's long hair about her shoulders and breasts. My God, I shouldn't have agreed to bring her along. What would Rosie think?

We passed some of the most venerable cabins on the lake, built when White Pine was the only resort, when boat races and fish derbies filled the summers and every Saturday night saw couples swaying to a live band at the Starlight Dance Pavilion. Now White Pine had lost much of its popularity to other recreational areas that had developed around the lake. One thing that had helped sustain the resort was the campground and trailer park, where I was headed.

I pulled into the cafe parking lot, intending to leave Juliette in the van and walk the rest of the way to the trailer park, a distance of about three hundred yards. It immediately proved to be a poor decision as looking into the car beside me, I saw the unsmiling face of Eleanor Evanisky. Her bovine eyes came to life when she caught sight of Juliette in the seat next to me. I couldn't have picked a worse person to park beside had I tried. Eleanor's reputation as a gossip was eclipsed only by that of Helen Mousie down at the Co-op Store.

"Hello, Eleanor," I croaked.

"Fancy meeting you here, Bart Bartowski." She said my name as if committing it to memory. "Who's your friend?"

Oh God. "Oh, yes. Eleanor, this is Juliette. She's staying down at Pebble Beach. I…uh gave her a lift." I looked over apologetically at Juliette.

"Hello," Eleanor said, clearly trying to evaluate the spice factor.

Looking past me, Juliette said, "Hello."

At this point I knew I had to do something, so I said through the side of my mouth so Eleanor wouldn't notice, "Go into the café," then added, "please," with some difficulty as the pl sound is not easy to enunciate without benefit of lips.

Juliette, bright girl that she was, grabbed her small pack, hopped out of the van, saying, "Thanks for the ride," and walked towards the café, waving briefly to Eleanor.

"Pretty girl," Eleanor said after watching Juliette's long legs take her efficiently into the café. She gave me a look that said *lecher*, then her window slid silently closed. She sat there looking a little lost, occasionally glancing from side to side.

There was nothing left but to carry on, so I walked over to the campground, passing the vacant lot where the dance pavilion once stood. Across from it, empty tenting sites waited patiently for summer to arrive. As I reached the trailer park, a vehicle heading toward the exit left a trail of dust behind. It didn't take long before I found the rusty, green pick-up. It was parked next to a classic Air Stream trailer, circa 1950. Boxes of empty beer bottles and other items waited in front of the trailer to be recycled, and an old ten-speed bike leaned against the twin propane tanks. A couple of rickety lawn chairs looked at each other a few feet from the door.

The trailer was backed well into the small thicket of trees that surrounded the site. There was no answer to my knock on the screen door. I knocked again. Still no response. "Hello," I said, "anybody home?"

When nobody answered I pulled the tarnished aluminum door open and peered in. The place was a mess. The floor was thick with the comings and goings of muddy boots, and every surface was littered with dirty dishes, cans and bottles. The springs complained as I mounted the two metal steps. As soon as I was inside, I knew there was something wrong. The bathroom door hung drunkenly by one hinge, the attached mirror was smashed, and shards of glass lay on the floor below. I moved toward it cautiously.

I flinched as the trailer moved suddenly. "Christ," I said, "you scared the hell outta me, Juliette. What are you doing here?"

"What is it?" She asked.

I turned toward the damaged door. "I don't know yet."

I only had to shift the door slightly to see a boot, then a jeaned leg and finally a whole body lying on the floor. The head was partly hidden behind the toilet. Blood had flowed into the centre of the small room, lots of blood.

Taking a deep breath, I said, "Juliette, get out of here. Now."

"What is it?" she repeated, poking her head around the broken door. "Oh no…" Her face turned pale, and just before she fainted away, I grabbed her around the waist. I managed to keep her head from hitting the kitchen counter top and let her down as gently as I could, given that she was no featherweight. I ran water into the cleanest glass I could find and poured some into her open mouth. Choking a little and coughing, she came out of the faint. I helped her out of the trailer and sat her down on one of the old lawn chairs.

"Just stay there," I said. "I've got to get to a phone." She swayed in the chair a little. "Are you okay?"

She blinked slowly. "I guess so."

"Okay, good. I'll be right back."

"You're not leaving me here are you?" she bleated, as I began to walk away. "I'm not staying here by myself."

"Yeah, I guess you're right," I said. "Come on." I helped her to her feet. She wobbled for a few steps, but soon we were picking up the pace along the gravel drive.

"Who is it?" she asked.

"I'm not sure, but I think it's Andy Meyer." ARM. Andrew Redding Meyer. I remembered the name well. I'd been screening applications the year we hired an assistant greens keeper and I found the name much more distinguished than the applicant turned out to be.

After depositing Juliette in the van, I called the RCMP from the phone booth outside the cafe. When Nettie answered, I asked for Fred Snell.

"He's not here right now, Bart, but you can talk to Constable Reed."

"Fine." When she came on, I couldn't help but use the line I'd heard so often in movies and on television, a line I never thought I'd ever use. "I want to report a murder," I said.

But even as I said it, I wondered if it was an accurate statement. Was it murder? What led me to believe that? I tried to remember what I'd actually seen. A man lying on the floor, the bathroom door nearly torn off its hinges. Maybe he'd had a heart attack or slipped and hit his head. Then a thought struck me…maybe he wasn't dead at all. Then I remembered the blood. Lots of blood. Blood running out from behind the base of the filthy toilet. Blood pooling in the middle of the room.

"I don't know if it was a murder," I said, "but I did find what I believe to be a dead body in Andy Meyer's trailer at White Pine Beach."

"Okay, just hold on."

There was silence on the line for a minute before another voice came on, a more casual, confident voice. "Mr. Bartowski, this is Sergeant Hutt. Please tell me where you're calling from."

"I'm calling from the payphone at White Pine Beach."

"All right. I want you to stay right where you are. Do not return to the trailer and please don't say anything to anybody. We'll be there in a few minutes. Do you understand?"

"Yes." I hung up and walked over to the van. Juliette's eyes followed me as I came around to the passenger side and opened the door. "How are you feeling now?" I asked.

"Okay, I guess," she said weakly.

"Can you walk? I mean, do you think you could walk back to your place."

She looked bewildered. "What do you mean? Shouldn't I stay here?"

"I just think it would be better if you weren't here. Simpler, you know." Simpler for me, I figured. Discovering a dead body is one thing, discovering a dead body in the company of a beautiful, minimally clad, young woman is something else again. "They don't need you," I said. "I can tell them what I found and that'll be that. There's nothing you can really add. And this way you won't have to be involved."

She looked uncertain. "I guess." She swung her legs out of the van and stood.

"You okay?"

"Yeah," she said without looking at me.

"Maybe this isn't such a good idea," I said, uncertainly, as she took a few steps away from me.

She glanced over her shoulder, a vacant look on her face. "It's all right," she said, "I'll go."

She had just disappeared around a bend in the road, when two police cars came flying down the highway, sirens blaring. Careening into White Pine, they came to a tire crunching halt a few feet away, showering me with dust.

9

————————

"Tell me again why you went to Meyer's trailer," Sergeant Hutt said.

After answering a few preliminary questions at the lake, I had waited in the police car and then waited some more at the station. Finally Hutt and Fred returned and began the formal questioning. By this time the conflicting stories I had running around in my head were getting confusing. I had worked out several scenarios of how I would keep Juliette's name out of it, but now I'd all but forgotten which one I was going to use. They could see the indecision on my face.

"What took you there, Bart?" Fred threw in when I didn't respond.

"Okay," I said with a sigh meant to indicate I was telling the truth, the whole truth and nothing but. "I needed to talk to Andy about some golf course business." The look on their faces was not encouraging.

"What business?"

"Oh, just some housekeeping stuff," I said.

Hutt looked over at Fred. "Go on."

"I drove out to White Pine and parked at the café."

"Why didn't you drive to Meyer's trailer?"

"It was a nice day, I felt like stretching my legs."

"Yes?"

"I walked over to the trailer park."

"To Meyer's trailer?"

"Yeah."

"And you went inside?"

"Well, first I knocked a few times and called through the screen door, but there was no answer. Then I went inside."

"What was your first thought upon finding the body?" Hutt asked.

"I don't know."

"You weren't surprised?"

"Of course I was," I protested.

"Okay."

"It didn't look like an accident."

"What led you to believe that?"

"The door nearly torn off its hinges. The blood. It just looked violent."

"Did you see anyone in the campground? Anybody walking? Any vehicles? Anyone in a hurry, for instance?"

A four-by-four streaked through my memory, a four or five year old Blazer. "No. Can't say as I did."

"Nothing?"

I shook my head.

"Okay, Bart. Let's go through this again," Hutt said.

Around eleven I drove the dark, deserted streets home. The porch light was on at my house and I found Rosie sleeping on the couch in the living room. I stroked her brow until her eyes opened.

"What happened?" She said, her voice drowsy.

"Nothing much. Come on, let's go to bed."

"Hold on." Rosie roused herself. "What did they ask you? Why did they keep you there so long?"

"After I called you, I waited 'till almost nine, then they asked questions for a couple of hours, and here I am." I helped her to her feet. "I'm tired, let's talk about it in the morning."

"Tell me one thing, Bart. Are you in any trouble?"

"Nothing like that. I found the body, so they wanted to get everything they could while it was still fresh in my mind. No," I said as much to convince myself as Rosie, "I'm not in any trouble. Come on, let's go to bed, eh."

After a restless few hours in the sack, I gulped several cups of strong coffee, then putting on overalls and my work boots, went out into the garden. A bracing prairie wind had blown in from the east, bringing with it a stinging intermittent rain. Despite the inclement weather, it would feel good to do some physical work. It was the first chance I'd had to get into the garden since being discharged from the hospital.

After pulling out everything that looked like a weed, I took the wheelbarrow over to the back of the shed where I'd stored a couple of hay bales under a tarp. I broke one of them open and filled the wheelbarrow. I began distributing the hay over the garden to serve as mulch. I did the same on the beds containing garlic, basil and tomato on the south side of the house. Mulching would help retain moisture and keep the weeds at bay while we were at the lodge.

I was about to head in to take the chill off with another hot cup of coffee, when Nick, driving his wife's Escort, pulled up in the alley behind the house. Getting out of the car, he paused and looked both ways before walking over to where I stood near the stair leading up to the back door.

"Cold mother, ain't it?" he said. "You'd think it was goddamn October." He pulled up the zipper on his jacket. "So, word has it you found Andy." He examined my face uneasily.

"Where'd you hear that?"

"I take it the word is true?" he said.

"Yup." I wanted to see Nick's reaction, so I said, "It was pretty grisly too. Blood pouring out of his head like it was a busted watermelon."

"Somebody must of hit him pretty damn hard," Nick said.

"I guess so." I kept my eyes on him. "I see you're driving Wilma's car."

"Yeah, she wanted to take the Blazer to work today. I guess there's some construction up that way, road's pretty rough."

"She take it yesterday too?"

Nick looked at me for a long moment. "No, no she didn't. Why do you ask?"

"Oh, no reason," I said vaguely.

"What are you getting at?"

"Nothing, it's just I saw a truck that looked an awful lot like yours leaving the trailer park yesterday, just before I found Andy's body."

"You're full of shit," he said.

"Okay, Nick, whatever you say." I pulled up my collar against the wind. "So, what do you want? Why'd you come over here?"

He looked off in the distance. "Wouldn't you fuckin' know it? I go out to see a guy..." Nick's whole body jerked as he said, "Jesus H. Christ."

"Just tell me what happened," I said.

"Yeah, well, fuck it." He looked up into the dull gray sky. The rain was coming down steadily now. "I might as well. I got nothing to lose, eh? I'm already accused of one murder. Why not two?"

"Remember, Nick, I'm on your side."

His naturally cheerful demeanor was gone. Like the day itself, there was nothing but gloom left on his face.

"I went to see Andy, eh," he said.

"What for?"

"He called and said he had something to tell me. Something that would prove I didn't kill Harvey."

Thunder crackled near by, and rumbled down the valley. I couldn't bring myself to ask the obvious question.

Nick detected my hesitation. "No, I did not kill Andy, if that's what you're thinking. He was already dead when I got there."

"Why did you take off?"

"Well, what would you expect me to do, hang around and wait for the cops to show up? And I'd have been outta there free and clear if you hadn't come along. What the hell were you doing out there, anyway?" he said, irritably. "Did you tell the bulls you saw me?"

Again I hesitated. I'm not sure why. Maybe I wanted to see how desperate he had become. Had he simply come upon the poor, unfortunate Andy Meyer?

"Well?" he persisted.

"No, Nick, I didn't tell them. For one thing, I wasn't sure it was your truck. I saw a truck that looked like yours, that's all." I'm not sure why I was justifying my recalcitrance with the police; after all, Nick was the last person that would judge me for it. I guess I was justifying it to myself. I knew I'd withheld some pretty condemning evidence.

Nick sat down dispiritedly on the stairs that led up to our small deck, the stairs that Rosie had been cawing about ever since they were built.

"What do you plan to do?" I asked.

"I don't know," he said.

Rosie kept a mental list of people who'd tripped, stumbled or even commented on the steps.

"There's only one choice," I said.

"There's always more than one," he said, "that's why they call it choice."

Granted, there had been a few mishaps on those stairs, but damned if I was going to replace a perfectly good stairway; it just led to the garden, after all.

"You ought to get these stairs fixed, you know that," Nick said.

"Not you too."

His eyes crinkled, showing deep laugh lines.

"How about a coffee?" I said, as I climbed past him up the steep stairway, but when I'd turned, he was already half way to the Escort.

"No thanks," he said, "gotta run."

10

Later, from down in my office, I caught a whiff of dinner. Rosie had promised me pork chops, thick, breaded chops, brown and crispy, served with mashed potatoes and sauerkraut.

Salivating freely, I felt my thigh muscles complain as I climbed up the steps from the bear pit. My injured knee protested only mildly. I was surprised to hear a siren, and it was obviously on our crescent. I assumed it was the ambulance coming to the seniors care home next door. Rosie and I had been very unhappy when the neighboring lot was filled with a long, dull gray house, lacking any redeeming aesthetic qualities, but even unhappier when we learned they'd somehow finagled a license to house the aged and infirmed. We assumed the worst, a constant parade of visitors, a lot of bewildered seniors wondering into the street, and a steady arrival of ambulances carting them off to the hospital or funeral parlour. But as it turned out, there was none of that. In fact, Ted and Henrietta turned out to be nice folks. Unbidden, Ted cleaned my driveway with his blower after heavy snowfalls. And we were happy to have the seniors around, they added a nice mix to the family oriented Canuck Crescent.

The siren turned out to be a police car, not an ambulance, nor was it going to the seniors' retirement centre. It pulled up with some haste and parked diagonally, as for some reason police cars tend to do, in my driveway. With the neighbors looking on, I was glad Fred had turned off the siren, although he did leave the lights flashing. He and Detective Klassen walked swiftly across the lawn toward the house.

In my sock feet, I opened the door.

Detective Klassen, in a voice designed to brook no objection, told me I was to accompany them.

But I did object. "I was just about to sit down to dinner."

"Did you hear what I said?" Klassen hissed through clenched teeth.

"What's this all about?" I appealed to Fred.

"What's going on?" Rosie said, entering the porch. "Bart?"

"I don't know," I said.

"Fred," Rosie said, "what's going on?"

"We need to talk to Bart," Fred Said. "It's about yesterday."

Klassen glowered at my stockinged feet. "Get your shoes on, and let's go."

"Bart," Rosie groaned. "You told me you weren't in any trouble?"

The two policemen ignored her.

"Am I under arrest, because if not, I'd like to have my dinner first." I could hear the pork chops sizzling in the frying pan.

To my surprise, Klassen grabbed my upper arm and began leading me out the door. I tried to pull away, but was immobilized when he wrenched my elbow and forced it behind me. Fred looked alarmed, but grabbed my work boots and followed. Rosie stood in the doorway, watching as they sat me in the back seat of the police cruiser. As we rolled out of the crescent, I could still smell those pork chops.

Sergeant Hutt sat in Fred's office and was in deep conversation with someone. I couldn't see who it was. Nor did my view improve when Klassen took me downstairs and stuck me in a cell. The only other jailbird was the town drunk who gave me a conspiratorial wink.

Fred came down a few minutes later shaking his head. "Bart, Bart, Bart," was all he said before escorting me upstairs where Hutt and Klassen waited.

The lines on Hutt's face were deeply drawn, and his eyelids sagged. He looked like he hadn't slept in a week. The pack of Du Mauriers in his shirt pocket was flattened.

"Do you want to tell us about it?" His voice, too, was tired.

"Tell you about what?" I feigned frustration.

"Mr. Bartowski," he said, feigning patience in return. "We spoke to Ms. Riskowsky."

I felt nauseous and my eyes began to water.

"We'd like to have you confirm what she told us."

I felt like I was again standing in the office of Principal Horchak, the scourge of Tommy Douglas High, who liked nothing better than to interrogate students before a gathering of teachers, there to watch the tyrant do what he did best.

"Do you realize that you may have compromised a murder scene because you didn't want to let on that you were with your girlfriend?"

"What the hell are you talking about," I said, "she's not my girlfriend."

"But you don't deny she was with you?"

"No," I said, "you obviously know already."

"Didn't you learn anything from your last experience at playing amateur detective?" Hutt said. "To hear you tell it, someone knocked you senseless, then pushed you into that ravine and left you for dead. Let me ask you this," he breathed audibly, "what if the killer had still been in the trailer? Do you think he would have hesitated to put you out of your misery too? And were you prepared to risk the life of the Riskowsky girl?"

"No, I wasn't," I tried to sound contrite, adding lamely, "I asked her to stay at the café."

Detective Klassen, his form fitting shirt as crisp as ever and his black shoes shiny, said, "You could be charged with interfering with a murder investigation and tampering with evidence. Do you know what that gets you?" He didn't wait for me to respond. "Two to five years, Buster, that's what."

"I wasn't interfering. I mean, I discovered a body, but I didn't touch anything. I just went and knocked on a guy's door, eh."

"The problem is," Sergeant Hutt said, "if you lied to us about Ms. Riskowsky, you may have lied to us about other things, and, given your penchant for amateur detecting, may have even removed items from the crime scene, or contaminated them in some way. Now, I put this to you in the gravest terms, and in view of the charges that will be brought against you if we find out otherwise: is there anything else you did not tell us about?"

God, this was getting dodgy, eh. Should I tell them that I saw Nick? Maybe someone else saw him too. Fuck it. I owed it to Nick. "No," I said, resolutely, "there's nothing else."

"That better be the goddamn truth, or we'll hang your ass out to dry, buddy." This from Klassen, who then walked over to the open door and nodded to Fred Snell. A few moments later I saw a downcast Juliette Riskowsky pass by on her way out of the detachment.

"Now, don't you have a fishing lodge to run?" Hutt said. "I'd like you to concentrate on fishing. Is that clear?"

"Yes," I said, "perfectly clear."

"Then I guess we're done here," Hutt said, getting up and reaching for his flattened pack of cigarettes.

"Do you have any idea who killed Andy?" I ventured.

His patience finally gone, Hutt said, "Good day, Sir."

On my way out of the police station, though feeling somewhat chastened, I couldn't help but notice a plastic bag on one of the desks in the outer office. There was an official looking sticker on it that I couldn't read, but inside was what looked like a wig, a red wig.

I decided to stick with my plan for the afternoon, which was to go to the marine shop and test my motors. I'd had occasions where repaired equipment was driven up two hundred miles, then at great expense flown another hundred to the lodge, only to find that it worked no better than before I took it into the shop. So, over the years I'd adopted a policy of shop testing equipment. That way, if there was still a problem, it'd be handled then and there, and not in the middle of Stuart Lake with clients who were paying big bucks, had a limited amount of time, and weren't that keen on spending it sitting in a broken down boat.

"How's it going Benny?"

Benny rolled out from under an eighteen foot Starcraft. "Yeah, hi Bart," he said, wiping what looked like clear epoxy off his hands. "Here for the motors?"

"Yeah. Let's test those suckers."

"Well, I don't know, eh, I'm pretty busy."

"You said we'd test them today. They're ready, aren't they?" Benny still hadn't looked at me. "I gotta get those things up north, my season starts in a few weeks. I got a million things to take care of before then. I can't muck around," I added good-naturedly.

Benny mumbled something that I couldn't quite make out.

"What was that?" I said.

He turned and walked over to the workbench.

"Sorry, I didn't hear you," I said. Still he didn't respond.

"What the hell's going on, Benny?"

"I don't think a family man should…"

"What?" I said. "What are you talking about?"

He turned to me and said, "I think you know, eh."

Then it hit me. Apparently word was out that I was with Juliette when I found the body. Like a bad smell, you can't keep news like that secret for long. No doubt Eleanor Evanisky, or for that matter, Nettie at the police station had let her rip. And here was Benny Langthorne, deacon of the Baptist church, making sure I got the message. That was exactly why I'd tried to avoid getting Juliette involved. Small towns, you gotta love 'em.

"I don't know what you heard, Benny," I said, "but I wouldn't jump to any conclusions if I were you. Now, can we test those motors, or not?"

Doubtless Rosie had been downtown and caught a whiff of the news. Taking the long way home, I mentally prepared for what might be waiting for me, but, had I driven to Saskatoon and back, I couldn't have prepared nearly enough.

In the driveway of my house sat Juliette's blue MG. What the hell was she doing here? I can tell you, I trod very tentatively up the front step and into my house. Seeing or hearing nothing, I crept through the kitchen then peered into the living room where I discovered my wife sitting next to a teary, runny-nosed Juliette Riskowsky.

When she saw me, Rosie said, "Bart, put some tea on, would you?" letting me know that my presence wasn't required at that moment and putting me in my place at the same time. From the kitchen, I could hear Juliette's murmurs mixed with Rosie's commiserating.

I took my time making the tea. I used Rosie's nicest tea service, the one the kids and I had given her for Mothers' Day one year. I added a plate of digestive cookies along with a few chocolate wafers. When it sounded like Juliette had calmed down some, I filled the teapot and went in with the tray. I set it down on the coffee table in front of the women. Neither of them looked at me. After more minutes of being ignored, I decided I might just as well pour the tea.

"Milk and sugar?" Rosie said picking up the cream pitcher.

"Just a little sugar," Juliette responded, a tiny smile curling her lip.

"Have a cookie."

"Thank you." Juliette chose one of the chocolate wafers, which crunched loudly when she took a bite off of it. She looked a little embarrassed as a few crumbs floated to the hardwood floor.

"So, Bart," Rosie said. "Juliette came here looking for you, and as you can see, she's quite upset." Juliette kept her eyes on the crumbs that lay at her feet. "You seem to have created quite a stink around town as well." Her voice wavered as she said, "I'd like to know what's going on."

Juliette never moved. Nor did I for that matter. But, I guess, by rights, it was my job. "Look, sweetheart," I said. That was obviously the wrong opening because Rosie gave me a look that would take paint off walls. "What I mean is," I said, "there's nothing going on. Juliette was helping me out, that's all."

"With what? Your snooping around, I suppose," she said with annoyance. "That's another issue I want to talk about. But first, I want to hear what Juliette has to say."

Oh God. Juliette sat there like a schoolgirl who'd been caught dipping into her parents' liquor cabinet. Her eyes and nose were red rimmed, and with her hair pulled back behind her ears, she looked nothing like the young woman who had so brazenly propositioned me the day before. And I was glad of it.

"Mrs. Bartowski, I'm sorry if you got the wrong impression. Trust me, there's nothing going on. Bart and I met when he came to my parents' cottage. When I saw that truck at Rileys, I called to let him know, that's all."

I knew what was going through Rosie's mind, so I added, "Juliette came along, but she was supposed to stay at the café while I went to Andy's trailer, but..."

"Bart tried to keep me out of it, but I was curious," Juliette volleyed. "Foolish, I know. The police ordered me to come to the station this morning, and that's when they said we'd been seen together." She looked at me apologetically. "I had to tell them the truth."

"They weren't too happy with me either," I said, trying to take the pressure off Juliette, "accused me of interfering with a police investigation. Damn near charged me for tampering with evidence."

"Listen to the two of you," Rosie said. "You sound like a couple of criminals. Accused, tampering, being forced to tell the truth. We are law-abiding citizens. We're friends with policemen. Why are you running around like some kind of outlaw, Bart? You almost got yourself killed once doing that. And how could you get this young woman involved? Do you want her to be next? Good God. I'm telling you this, you had better smarten up, the both of you, if you don't want to end up in jail, or dead. And Bart..." Just then Stuart stormed in from school making one heck of a racket. "Oh..." she shook with anger, "pour some more tea."

"Where's my snack?" Stuart shouted as Rosie went out to the kitchen.

"How'd I do?" Juliette whispered.

"What are you doing here?" I whispered back.

"I came to see you, to talk to you."

"What's to talk about? We got caught. My big plan didn't work. Didn't work worth a shit. Listen, I'm sorry I got you into this."

"You didn't. I asked to go along, remember?"

"Are you on your way back to the lake?" I asked in hopes she'd take the hint.

"No, I'm going into the city. Things just feel too weird around here. Besides I've got spring semester starting soon." With a hopeful expression on her face, she whispered, "Maybe we could get together in the city."

"I think you better go," I whispered back, and just then we noticed that Stuart had parked himself at the entrance to the living room.

"Why are you guys whispering?" he asked. "Mom, why are these guys whispering?" he tossed back into the kitchen, where Rosie was preparing his snack.

Juliette jumped up and headed for the door, patting Stuart on the head as she passed him. I heard her say goodbye and Rosie's curt response, then the front door and finally Juliette's car starting and driving away.

I waited for the deluge. And I waited some more. Nothing. This could be worse than I thought. I carried the tea tray into the kitchen. Stuart was busy munching away at peanut butter on toast while Rosie stood in stony silence, staring out the window.

I dutifully placed the tea things in the dishwasher while Stuart helped himself to more peanut butter. "So, how was school?" I asked him.

At the sound of my voice, Rosie turned and walked stiffly out of the room. I could hear her resolute steps thunder down the long hallway to our connubial bedroom. The door slammed with a certain irrevocability.

"I think you're in trouble, Dad," Stuart said, before taking another huge bite of his toast.

I spent a fitful night on the lumpy couch in the loft, trying to keep out of Rosie's way, but not before I had made supper for Stuart and me, cleaned up the kitchen to perfection and even started plans for rebuilding those damned stairs that Rosie was so pissed about. I left the plans on the kitchen table in hopes that seeing them might brighten her outlook a little.

11

_____

"Well," Dee Elliot said when I stepped into the newspaper office on Main Street, "if it ain't our very own Magnum, P.I.?" Dee owned the *Crooked Lake Reporter,* and had run it ever since the death of her father, who'd edited the paper for some twenty-five years.

"Morning, Dee," I said. Shooting the breeze with Dee was one of life's small pleasures.

She wore a pair of men's work pants and a faded sweatshirt from Crooked Lake's homecoming. "How're you doing?" she said.

"Not bad, considering." I felt a little embarrassed about the whole Juliette affair.

"Yeah, I heard all about it from Helen," Dee chuckled.

I tried to keep from blushing.

"Do you think Andy's murder is connected to Harvey somehow?" she asked.

I squinted at her as though it were too painful to speculate on.

"Come on in and sit down," she said. I walked behind the counter to where a couple of desks sagged under the weight of stuff desks seem to accumulate. Dee and I sat across from one another. She put a boot up on the edge of the desk. Based on the fact that she had never married, was a rabid football fan, and lumbered around town in an old three-quarter-ton truck, some assumed Dee was of that other persuasion.

"We both know there's been a lot of bad blood out at the park," she said. Dee had written more than one scathing editorial on the subject. "But I can't imagine who would want to kill Andy Meyer, or why?" She took another sip of coffee. "According to the cops, it was done by some strong bugger. Well, you would know. You were there."

"Yeah, I was there," I said soberly.

Dee shoved some litter to one side of her desk and picked up a pencil. "So?"

"So what?"

"So what did you see?"

"I don't think the police would appreciate a description of their crime scene on the front page of *the Reporter*," I said. "I'm in enough trouble with them already."

"It's news, Bart. The public's got a right to know."

"And what about my rights?" I said. "What if I'm not interested in telling the story?"

Dee watched a giant tractor take up several parking spaces in front of the Co-op Store. "Okay. I'll ask the questions and any time it gets too prickly, don't answer. How's that?"

"Dee, I didn't come here to be interviewed."

Dee and I actually agreed on a lot of things, and valued one another's opinion. Her Dad had been a real advocate for the little guy and she had kept up the family tradition. But, so as not to lose advertisers, she left out diatribes about what she called the tax-cutting, free-trade-loving, bigger-business-is-better regimes in both Regina and Ottawa.

"Okay, fine, let's just talk," she said flatly.

"Well, here it is," I said. "Not a murder in Crooked Lake for decades, and now two in less than a month. People must be getting pretty upset, right? What are they saying?" A small town newspaper editor often has the pulse of the community, and Dee was no exception.

"I thought this wasn't an interview," she said, dryly.

"I'm just wondering if people are talking," I said.

"Oh, people are talking all right. They're talking up a storm about the weather, fuming about the high price of gas, complaining about their neighbours, the government, you name it."

"What's new about that?"

"Nothing. It's just that very little is being said about the murders. It's as though people want to force it out of their minds with everyday babble. The more mundane crap they can fill their heads with, the less they have to think about what happened. People don't want to acknowledge that someone in their community had the devil in his soul, had enough hate, enough ugliness to murder one of their own, much less two. They don't know who to trust and frankly I think they're scared."

"Do you think they have reason to be," I said.

She reached for her thermal Roughriders coffee cup. "I know I wouldn't let my kids out at night, if I had any." She took a sip of coffee, made a face and pulled out her pencil. "You know, I think I've got an idea for next week's editorial."

"I better get going," I said.

"What's the rush?"

"I don't want to be part of next week's editorial, and besides, I'm getting ready for the season. Got a lot to do."

"I'm gonna make it up there one of these years," she said. Dee had been promising to come fishing, but as yet hadn't made it to the lodge, usually spending her holidays in Vancouver or San Francisco.

"Thanks for the chat," I said.

"Come and see me anytime," Dee said with a Mae West drawl. Even as I stepped through the door she was busy writing.

I walked across the street to the post office. Les Thatcher stood behind the counter, glasses set low on the bridge of his nose, he was gazing into a big ledger.

"Hey, Les," I said, startling him.

"Bart..." He removed his glasses, then closing the ledger, said, "I hear you found Andy Meyer, that right?"

I made a face of assent that reflected something of how I felt about having discovered a dead body.

Les ignored the look and went on, "Jesus, what did he look like?"

"Well, he was kind of just lying there, dead you know."

"I heard there was lots of blood," Les persisted.

"I'd rather not talk about it, Les."

But by this time a small crowd was gathering. Mrs. Zimmer, a short, stout widow with a foghorn voice that could be heard as far as the Alberta border said, "I hear Andy's brother is in town from Zenita and he's looking for the one that did it."

I tossed some junk mail into the recycling box.

"Who do you think did it?" Les asked me, ignoring the fact that I was half way out the door.

"I don't think it was anybody here, was it?" I looked from face to face inquiringly. People were uncomfortable at first, then got the joke. I could still hear Mrs. Zimmer's resounding guffaws as I opened the door to Rosie's van.

Since it was a few minutes before the noon bell, I decided to drive by the school. Maybe it was because of what Dee had said. A flood of kids came out the door and Stuart was among them. I tooted my horn staccato-like to get his attention. He looked around, then made his way out of the stream of students.

"Hi, Dad. What're you doing here?"

"Oh, just passing by, thought I'd see if you wanted a ride."

"Sure."

As we drove home, I asked him, "Any talk about Andy Meyer in school?"

"Not much, but somebody said his brother is going to find out who did it, and maybe...kill him."

"Do you believe that?"

Stuart squinted into the noonday sun. "No way," he snorted. "That's like some kind of western movie." He mimicked a Texas twang, "You killed my brother, now I'm gonna kill you."

We drove in silence for another block. "How're you doing with all this?" I asked.

"I don't know," Stuart said. "I don't think about it too much." He fiddled with the zipper on his lightweight baseball jacket. "But I don't want you to get hurt anymore."

Before I could respond, he rolled down the window and waved to old Mr. Bittel who sat out on his front porch sunning himself. Joe Bittel, to whom Rosie often sent meals, had lost his wife a year before and was just now coming out of it. In fact this was the first time I'd seen him outside the house this spring. While his wife was alive they would have been in the yard as soon as the snow was gone, trimming the shrubs and preparing the flowerbeds, but Joe hadn't touched a thing yet.

Rosie was back at her old station in front of the stove, a one-woman whirlwind. She had short ribs roasting in the oven, potatoes boiling and vegetables steaming. On the table was a big green salad waiting to be tossed. "Wash your hands, Stuart," she said, "dinner will be on the table in a few minutes."

She ignored me.

"Rosie," I said, "how long are you going to keep this up?"

She didn't respond.

"Rosie," I protested.

"That's up to you," she said.

Now, what was I supposed to say to that? Stuart returned to the kitchen and sat down.

"You've got cadets tonight," Rosie said.

"I know."

"Is your uniform ironed?"

"Yes."

"Your boots polished?"

"Of course." These were unnecessary questions as Stuart was meticulous when it came to his uniform and sported numerous merit badges to prove it. "Man, that smells good," he said as Rosie set a heaping plate in front of him.

While he dug in, I went to the stove and began serving myself.

Rosie sat at the table grilling Stuart about his morning at school, which he hated. He always said, "How can I eat if I have to be answering a lot of dumb questions?"

But a half hour later, he was on his way back to school, and it was my turn in the hot seat.

"How is it that everyone in town is talking about you and that girl? How old is she anyway?" Rosie didn't wait for answers. "Don't you care about your reputation? Don't you care about this family? Don't you love me?" Her eyes searched mine, seeking reassurance.

"Of course, I love you," I said. "I don't know what you've heard, but none of its true, believe me. My only involvement with Juliette was...well you know what it was. I don't dispute she's an attractive young woman, anyone can see that." Perhaps not the best thing to say in my defense. "But, I have no intentions toward her, nor do I plan to see her again. Rosie, please. This is crazy. You know I'm devoted to this family."

"You sure have a strange way of showing it."

I took a deep breath to calm myself. "I'm doing what I can to help my friend," I said. "Is that so bad? I've known Nick all my life. And I'm not doing this for kicks, or because I'm bored."

"Then why are you doing it?"

"Because I owe it to him."

"What do you mean? What do you owe him?"

I told her how Nick had saved my life that day on the lake.

"You've never once talked about this," Rosie said

"I know."

"Why?"

"I don't know. It's just between Nick and me, I guess."

"But it doesn't mean you have to sacrifice your family or yourself, does it?"

"No. But I can't give up on Nick. He saved me that day, and now it's my turn."

Rosie sat at the kitchen table worrying the end of her apron string, her eyes brimming with tears now. I wanted to take her in my arms, tell her everything was going to be all right, but I didn't and her tears retreated, unshed.

My old half-ton had been at Ernie's ever since he'd winched it out of Ireland's Ravine. Ernie ran the Esso station on Highway Four, and like most small town garage owners, did everything from pumping gas to pulling engines, and in Ernie's case, bodywork too. I was confident he'd have no problem setting my truck back on its feet.

There were a few vehicles parked next to the garage, among them a vintage, but obviously restored truck nearly like mine. The chrome was all shined up and it had been painted a nice two-tone blue. I could only hope that my truck looked half as good.

"Boy, that's a beauty out there," I said to Ernie nodding in the direction of the parking lot. "That's a sixty-nine too, right?"

"Yup, sure is," Ernie responded. His mechanic, Lefty Holdner, emerged from the vehicle bay, wiping grease off his hands.

"Is my old heap ready to go?"

"Yup, sure is," Ernie repeated to the seeming delight of his mechanic who had put down his rag and was leaning on the counter, grinning.

"So, where you got 'er?"

Now both of them were grinning. Ernie raised his chin in the direction of the restored half-ton outside the window. "It's been sitting there for two days."

A bewildered expression must have swept across my face, because the two of them began laughing, Lefty Holdner almost hysterically.

"Wait a minute," I said, "you're not saying that's my truck out there?"

My truck had rust eating away at it, dings and dents everywhere, all the things that thirty odd years of use and abuse will do to a half ton truck, plus the damage of rolling it down that ravine. Now it looked pretty much like it did when I drove it off Morris Teschuck's lot.

"I just knocked out a few dents, put in a new windshield and gave her a paint job."

It was obvious he'd done a whole lot more than that. We stepped outside and I circled the truck, examining it up close. Always thrift conscious, I asked, "What's this going to cost me?"

"Like I said, I didn't do that much," Ernie said.

Ernie and Vera Haidu had arrived in Crooked Lake without much to their name. Ernie was operating out of a single car garage at the back of his rented house and I'd had him do some repairs on this very truck. Pleased with the work, I started encouraging other people to take their vehicles to him. Before long Ernie was able to buy the Esso service station on the highway.

"Have a look under here," Lefty said. As he popped the hood, I noticed Harvey Kristoff's SUV arrive at the motel across Highway Four. The forest green Mercedes had been Harvey's pet. Unable to find just what he'd wanted at any of the Saskatoon dealerships, he'd traveled all the way to Winnipeg to buy the ML 500.

I could have sworn I was seeing Harvey hop out of the driver's seat, but it was his brother, Carl. We hadn't seen much of him since high school. In fact, the funeral was probably the first time I'd seen him since then. Actually he had come back for his dad's funeral a few years earlier, but we'd heard that a disagreement arose between the two brothers over the old man's estate. It sounded like Carl had got the short end of the stick. He left right after the funeral and hadn't been back since. Apparently he'd tried to sue Harvey, but I didn't know if anything had come of it. The brothers never were that close, even as kids. I watched Carl go into a unit at the end of the long, bungalow-style motel.

"We had to replace a few hoses," Lefty said, "and reconnect some things, but the engine's in pretty good shape." Ernie had rebuilt it a few years earlier.

"Man, you guys did one hell of a job," I said, my elbows leaning on the shiny, robin's egg blue fender.

As we stood there, an RCMP cruiser pulled up to the pump. Fred Snell got out of the car and walked over. "Truck's ready, I see," he said.

"Looks great, doesn't it?" I said.

Fred examined it.

Tensing a little, Lefty headed back into the station. He'd had his own scrapes with the law over the years.

"Fred, I wanted to ask you something," I said. "It's about the accident, you know the one I *didn't* have." His look was not encouraging, but I soldiered on. "It occurred to me that even a drunk would try to avoid hitting the ditch, wouldn't he?"

Fred straightened his cap and watched me, his face non-committal.

"Out at the ravine, it looked to me like my truck had simply rolled off the road. There were no skid marks or any indication that I'd done anything to prevent it. Now, does that sound right?"

"I'd say in most cases you'd see some sliding or braking, either at the point of entry or on the shoulder," he said. "However, if the driver were totally out of it or had fallen asleep…"

"Or had been knocked unconscious," I said.

His lower lip protruded doubtfully, then seeing Ernie replace the cap on the cruiser's gas tank, he walked over to the pumps. After signing the chit, he opened his car door and said, "Sorry, Bart. We've got bigger fish to fry right now."

12

_____

In light of the second murder, the police were re-examining the whole investigation. Word had it that Fred Snell, Hutt and Klassen along with two Crown prosecutors had gone into a huddle that lasted hours and pointed in every direction. According to Nettie, my name even came up, until Fred managed to convince them that I was just a busy body who happened to be in the wrong place at the worst time.

As a member of the park board, I had seen Andy Meyer at meetings and run into him at the golf course from time to time, but I hadn't known him well. I wasn't sure if anyone had, he was something of a loner. As for what he was doing at Riley's Rest, I had no idea, but I suspected his presence there was connected to Harvey somehow. I drove over to Nick's to see if he could shed some light on the enigmatic Andy Meyer.

Nick's house was deserted, but a block down I noticed Lloyd Hughes riding a mower around a small patch of grass in his front yard. Lloyd had been Harvey's main ally on the park board.

In response to my inquiry about Andy's off-season activities, Lloyd said, with a hint of the English accent left over from his childhood, "Haven't the slightest idea."

"How long had he been here?"

"It was five years on May first." Lloyd was a stickler for dates. "I recall, because that's the same spring we started work on the new underground sprinklers." He turned off the mower's engine and got out of the hydraulic seat. Pointing to the patio, he said, "Let's get out of this sun."

We sat down on comfortable chairs under a giant green umbrella that had the same logo stamped on it as the lawn mower. Lloyd poured us each a glass of lemonade from a frosty glass pitcher. I guess good manners were also left over from his English childhood.

"I never really saw Andy off the course," he said, "except at the odd board meeting or playing VLTs at the pub." Video Lottery Terminals were introduced into bars as a means of shoring up the flagging economy. Now the lonely, the addicted and the drinking poor were all glued to the silent bloodsuckers in every little watering hole in the province.

"He must have had some friends?" I said.

"He never struck me as the type who would have many friends," Lloyd said. "Kind of a Fats Rodnicki type." Fats had been one of those unfortunates who was, as the nickname implied, fat, not too bright, and socially inept. Always on the outside, looking in. He jumped off a bridge in Edmonton a few years back. Didn't leave a note.

The mention of Fats took us back to high school days. We exchanged reminiscences about other people we'd known and speculated on what had become of them. Harvey's name didn't come up.

Back on his mower, Lloyd pressed the start button and the motor hummed confidently to life.

"I wonder if Andy had any enemies," I said

"He must have had at least one," Lloyd said, over the engine's muffled growl.

News of Gerald Meyer had spread quickly. His first act had been to bully the police into admitting they had no suspects or any discernible motive and had recovered no murder weapon. After leaving the police station, Gerald had gone to the Co-op Store, apparently to stock up on grub. Naturally he crossed paths with Helen Mousie, and the two were seen at the pub together later that evening.

Despite what I'd heard, I wanted to get next to Andy's brother and figured who better to grease those wheels than Helen. So I went down to the Co-op Store. We needed a few things anyway, always the case when you have an active twelve-year-old at home.

I caught Helen's eye at the cash register and waved her over to the produce section as though I had a question about the limp lettuce. She trundled over, and was puffing by the time she reached me. Helen was a big woman. Big in the hip, big in the chest, even big in the head where she stored all those rumours, half-truths, innuendoes and even the odd fact.

"How are you?" I said as casually as I could.

"Just fine, Bart."

I knew all I had to do was wait, so I just squeezed a mushy tomato. How I longed for vegetables from my own garden.

"Have you heard that Andy Meyer's brother is in town?" she asked.

Bingo. "Yeah," I said, "I guess I did hear something about that."

"He tied on a pretty good one down at the pub last night," Helen said. I feigned indifference. "Got pretty riled up too. He was accusing anyone and everyone of murdering Andy. By the by," she smiled demurely, "he mentioned your name."

"He did?" My cool façade waned. "What did he say about me?"

"Said maybe you did it. Said you coulda killed him, then called the cops to cover your heine."

"The guy's obviously got a wild imagination."

"You got that straight," she said. "He even accused me. That's when I went home." Helen raised her hand to pat the bun on the back of her large head, a coy gesture that left no doubt that she knew something you didn't. But before long, she was spilling everything she knew and probably some of what she didn't about Gerald T. Meyer. The T. apparently stood for Tiger, which referred to his on-ice antics, mimicking an infamous NHL fisticuffer, Tiger Williams.

Gerald bragged to Helen that he'd once taken on half the team from Balgonie in a particularly fight-filled hockey game. During the melee, Gerald claimed to have broken an arm, a couple of noses and left at least one dipsy-doodling centreman unconscious.

I was beginning to understand Gerald T.'s disposition and began to wonder at the wisdom of meeting him face to face. Helen told me he was staying at the motel.

The Crooked Lake Motel, while a little run down, is clean and provides the only beds in town other than the Shatski's B & B, and somehow I didn't think Gerald T. would be welcome there. The manager was out and the girl at the motel counter got wide-eyed when I asked for Gerald's room. I didn't bother to ask why, I could guess.

Nosed in dangerously close to the door of unit eight was a four-by-four pick-up, tires mounted on a severely jacked-up chassis, huge roof lights, and mudguards displaying a woman's disproportionate silhouette. Caked in mud, the vehicle brought to mind the road warriors at monster truck events who delight in bending, breaking and generally busting up everything in sight.

After several knocks followed by closed-fisted, albeit gentle, thuds on the door, I heard some grunting from within. A minute later a burly, unshaven brute of a man wrapped in a bed sheet opened the door. He squinted at the eleven AM sunshine that poured into his room.

"Gerald Meyer?" I said affably.

"Who the hell are you?" He hefted up the slipping bed sheet that had begun to reveal a generous spare tire.

"My name is Bart Bartowski and I…"

"You're the one that found Andy."

"Yes, that's right. I would like to offer my condolences." His glower softened a little. "I'm very sorry for your loss," I said. "He was a good man."

Grief competed with scorn on Gerald's grisly face. A tear threatened to escape one sleepy eye. Perhaps he was more than just the raging bull he'd been made out to be?

Fifteen minutes later, Gerald joined me in the motel's restaurant.

"Coffee, and keep it coming," he growled at the waitress. When she returned with his coffee, he ordered the Big Boy Breakfast, adding a tall stack of pancakes and a side of bacon to go with the six strips that came with it.

After he had guzzled two cups of coffee, Gerald now looked almost awake.

"Are you planning to stay around town for a while?" I asked.

"Long enough to find out who killed my brother," he said, "that's how long."

"Did you talk to the police?"

"Oh, yeah. They won't fuck with Gerald T., I'll tell you that much."

"What did they have to say?"

"They didn't have nothin' to say." He implied that he'd given them a hard time about it, too.

"Are you saying they weren't saying or they had nothing to say?"

"What?" He looked at me kind of puzzled, probably distracted as the Big Boy et al began to arrive, filling both his and my side of the small table.

"What I mean is…"

"I know what you mean," he interrupted. "They don't know nothin'." He shoved half an egg into his mouth. "Haven't got a clue." He chewed with his mouth open, sucking in air. He gulped some coffee, then said, "What were you doing at his place, anyway?"

I wasn't quite ready for that, so I took a long sip of my cold coffee. "I'm on the park board," I said, unable to come up with anything better, "and I had some business to talk over with him."

"What kinda business?" He flooded his pancakes with imitation maple syrup.

"Just some golf course stuff."

He ignored that. "The way I hear it, you been doing some sniffin' around of your own."

"Is that what you heard?"

"Yup." His eyes accused me while he drained his third scalding cup of coffee. "The way I hear it," he said, "you almost got yourself killed for your trouble."

"Well," I stalled, "you're pretty well informed." Helen Mousie, I swore silently.

He slathered several pats of butter over his pancakes then ate in silence, making short work of his tall stack.

"Did he ever talk to you about the golf course?" I asked, trying to catch him when his mouth wasn't full.

"Why?"

"Did he ever mention any problems?"

Gerald pushed his chair back from the table as if to allow more room for his discernibly expanding belly. Ignoring the *No Smoking* decal pasted to the wall next to our table, he took out a non-filtered Export A and lit up.

I watched his still-puffy eyes as he said in an oddly animated voice, "Yeah, he did by Jesus, he said he had a problem with some son-of-a-bitch by the name of Bartowski." A big grin slowly covered Gerald T.'s grisly mug and a wheezy rumble of laughter commenced somewhere deep inside that huge belly, it never did fully manifest, just stayed down deep like a volcano, threatening, but not yet ready to blow.

He took a deep drag on his cigarette and his face took on that grief-stricken look again.

"Understand you play a little hockey," I said.

"Yeah, a little," he said, as if he were Tiger Woods saying he played a little golf.

"Still play?" I asked.

"I've still got the moves, but I put on a few pounds," he patted his belly, "slowed me down some. You play?"

Just as we were getting into some major hockey banter, Fred Snell walked in. I could tell he wasn't a bit happy to see me in the company of Gerald T.

"Morning, Mr. Meyer. Bart."

I returned his greeting. Gerald just sat there looking morose.

"I need to talk to you for a minute," Fred said to Gerald.

Again Gerald ignored him.

"I'd like you to come down to the detachment to sign for your brother's personal belongings. I also need a little more information. With your cooperation, I'm sure we can handle this in a few minutes."

"What kinda information?" Gerald said.

Fred looked at me as if to will me away from the table. I didn't move. "For instance," he said, "are there other surviving family members?"

I watched something indiscernible wash over Gerald's face just before he snarled, "I don't suppose you guys know any more than you did yesterday?"

"You'll have to talk to Sergeant Hutt about that," Fred said. "He's in charge of the investigation."

"So what are you, just the messenger boy?" Gerald looked at me as if I shared his contempt for Fred.

"Mr. Meyer," Fred's voice was tight, "I'm in charge of the detachment here, and everything that goes on is my responsibility. Now, when can you make yourself available?"

"All right, all right, don't get your shit in a knot, eh," Gerald said loud enough for even the kitchen staff to hear, "you might pop one of those shiny buttons."

I couldn't help but smile at the forced restraint showing on Fred's face.

"And Bart," Fred said, not happy to see that I found this amusing, "I'd like to talk to you outside for a minute."

Under his breath, Gerald said, "Fuck'm if he can't take a joke."

Pretending I hadn't heard, I said, "I'll see you again."

"You know it," he shot back.

As we stepped out of the restaurant, Fred turned on me. "What the hell are you doing?"

"What are you talking about?"

"You know damned well what I'm talking about."

"I was offering my condolences to a guy who just lost his brother," I said. "Isn't that the neighborly thing to do?"

"I know what you're up to."

"Fred, just confirm one thing for me," I said. "You found a wig in Andy's trailer, right?"

"Damn you, Bartowski. How did you know that?"

"I saw it lying on a desk at the police station."

"You know, Bart, you have a way of getting into things that don't concern you." Fred turned and as he walked towards his car he said, "Just leave the policing to the police."

"Fine," I said. "But you might be interested to know that I saw that wig somewhere else."

Fred stopped dead in his tracks and turned. "And where was that?"

"At Riley's Rest."

"When?"

"The day of my so-called accident."

"And why didn't you tell us this before?"

"Because it didn't seem important. Now, I'm not so sure."

13

"Bart... Bart wake up."

When I opened my eyes, Rosie was shaking me.

"You were dreaming," she said.

After lunch, I'd lain down for my afternoon nap. Maybe it was the deep fried chicken, or the garlic olives Rosie liked to put in the potato salad, but I had one hellacious dream.

"What were you dreaming about?" Rosie asked as we sat at the kitchen table waiting for the kettle to boil.

"Golf."

"Golf?"

"You and I were golfing with Nick and Wilma. There was a foursome behind us, and they kept inching closer. We'd be taking our second shots and they'd already be teeing off. At each hole they'd get closer. On the fourth I could see it was Harvey and Andy and those two detectives."

"Sounds more like a nightmare to me," Rosie said.

"When we got to the seventh green, they were real close. All of a sudden Nick went running towards the water as though he were on fire, and just before he jumped in, a shot rang out and he crumpled like a rag doll on the water's edge. We stood there shocked. Finally Wilma ran towards Nick, but before she could reach him, Klassen and Hutt grabbed her. When I looked back to the tee, Harvey and Andy had disappeared. I started shouting after them…"

"Yeah," Rosie said, "I heard you from down in the laundry room for pity sake."

I shook myself to get the disturbing images out of my head. "Rosie, how about a nice veggie omelet for supper?"

After calming down over a cup of tea, I was reading about Canada's diamond boom in Maclean's Magazine when Rosie opened the door to a distraught Wilma Taylor. From my perch in the loft, I listened to their exchange.

"Oh Rosie, I don't know what to do."

"What's happening?" Rosie asked.

"Now they're saying he killed Andy Meyer."

"Who?"

"Nick," Wilma said, as though Rosie were dense.

"Now just slow down a minute," Rosie cautioned.

I eased myself off the couch and stood leaning on the railing.

Wilma spotted me. "Oh, Bart, it's like a nightmare. The kids are…they're convinced their father's a killer, especially now."

"What do you mean?" I said.

"I don't know where Nick is. I haven't seen him since yesterday morning."

The news was on the front page of *the Star-Phoenix* the following morning.

Nick Taylor, forty-one, currently out on bail for the murder of Harvey Kristoff is being sought in connection with the death of Andrew Meyer who was found dead in his trailer at White Pine Beach two days ago.

Andrew Meyer had been assistant greens keeper under Taylor at the Crooked Lake Regional Park and Golf Course for the past five years. Crooked Lake RCMP, cooperating with investigating officers from Saskatoon had little to say, but speculation has it that Meyer might have been silenced to prevent him from bringing forward evidence in the Kristoff case.

Taylor's wife Wilma said that her husband is innocent and has been falsely accused. When asked about his whereabouts, she refused to comment.

"So the paper says Mr. Taylor did it," Stuart said, sitting in front of his computer playing one of his kill everybody games.

"No it doesn't," I said, looking at my watch. "Why aren't you in school?"

"Professional day."

"Again. You just had Easter holidays."

"Dad, that was over a month ago."

"Well, then why don't you come out and help me in the garden?"

"'Cause there's nothing to do out there. You've already done it all."

"What about the grass?"

"Lawnmower's broken."

"Again?"

"Are they going to hang Mr. Taylor?" Stuart said over the sound of machine gun fire.

"We don't hang people in Canada."

"Yeah, but if somebody kills two people..."

"It doesn't matter, they still don't get hanged. We abolished capital punishment long ago."

He stopped clicking and looked up at me. "So, no matter how many people you kill you never get hanged?"

"That's right. Just like your game there."

He frowned at that. "I wish we lived in Texas, they hang everybody there."

"Stuart," I protested. Whose kid was this, anyway?

"Well, I think people should pay for their crimes. Not just sit around in a comfortable jail watching TV and eating steaks paid for by my taxes."

"They don't eat steaks, and you don't pay taxes."

"Yeah, but I will. Life imprisonment. That's what you get, right. Twenty-five years I'll be paying to keep Mr. Taylor in jail."

"No you won't."

"Yes I will. By the time I'm twenty, I'll be paying taxes and he'll still be in jail, in the pen."

"No he won't, Stuart. He won't go to jail because he didn't do it," I said.

"You think so, Dad?" Stuart looked hopeful.

"Yes I do, son," I said as more animated characters were slaughtered on the screen.

Talk on coffee row that morning was naturally about the article in the paper. Close to a dozen people, mostly men, sat at the horseshoe shaped counter.

"So, looks like Taylor took off," offered a heavyset farmer wearing green overalls and a John Deere cap.

"He's flown the coop," added Bill Bird, the retired teacher who frequented the Junction Stop and never failed to protract a metaphor.

"Why would he take off like that?" inquired the farmer.

"Whaddaya think," another speaker waded in—the gas jockey who was on a break from the pumps.

But before he could continue, the teacher declared, "An innocent man doesn't run." He challenged me with an even stare.

"That'll have to be proven in court," said the farmer, lifting the bill of his John Deere cap so he could scratch his bald head. His forehead was snow white.

"That will happen soon enough," Bill said with confidence.

"Well it better," added the gas jockey. "We don't want no murderer running around loose."

"That's an unfortunate double negative." The teacher couldn't help himself. The gas jockey just looked puzzled and the farmer went on scratching his head.

Finishing my coffee, I was about to leave when Bill said, "I see Ernie brought your old truck back to life." There were a few sniggers and averted eyes around the counter.

"Yeah, he did," I said. "Too bad he couldn't do the same for Harvey and Andy Meyer." The gas jockey's puzzled look returned. I twisted on my stool and walked out.

I drove over to the police station. In response to my query about progress in Nick's case, Nettie said, "Sorry, Bart, that information is hush-hush, except to his lawyer of course." Then she added in an undertone, "And he happens to be in there right now."

Corporal Klassen and Frank Hendrickson came out of one of the offices a few minutes later. I exchanged blank looks with the lawyer before he walked out.

"Just the man I wanted to see," Sergeant Hutt said, entering through the back door of the building. "Could we have a word?"

I followed him into Fred's office where they'd questioned me the night of Harvey's murder. Klassen followed as though I might try to make a break for it. Apparently Sergeant Hutt had just had a Du Maurier because the acrid smell emanating off him quickly fouled the small room.

"I need to go over a couple things with you," Hutt said, "and I need you to be straight with me." He looked at me forcefully. "We have a witness who puts Nick Taylor in the vicinity of White Pine Beach at the time of Meyer's murder."

I returned his forceful look with a puzzled one.

"Did you see Taylor at the trailer park that day?" He watched closely for my reaction, as did Detective Klassen who stood at-ease directly behind Sergeant Hutt.

"No, I didn't see him."

"Did you see his truck?"

I'd thought about answering this question before and there was no point trying to cover it up. After all, I knew damn well Nick had been there. "I saw a four or five year old Blazer leaving the trailer park as I arrived," I said. "I couldn't see it clearly because of the dust, so I can't say for sure whether it was Nick's truck or not."

Skepticism hovered over Hutt's face while something close to disgust perched on Klassen's.

"Okay, let's go back to Riley's cottage," Hutt said. I sensed Klassen bristling in anticipation. "Describe what you saw there."

I twisted my wedding band, setting the three small diamonds face up. "Well, I walked in...the door was open. There were papers on the kitchen table and some beach toys in one bedroom. There were some men's toiletries in the other bedroom and a suitcase in the closet with some stuff up on the shelf. That's the last thing I remember seeing, and it wasn't all that clear."

"What stuff was up on the shelf?" Sergeant Hutt asked, wriggling in his seat as though his pants were too tight. Before I could answer, he said, "What do you know about a red wig?"

"I remember seeing it here the day you dragged me away from my pork chops and sauerkraut."

"And where else have you seen it?"

"Well, if it's the same one, I guess I saw it at Riley's cottage the day I got clobbered."

"Why didn't you tell us this before?" Klassen said.

"I didn't remember it then."

"And why didn't you tell us about it when you did remember?"

"It didn't seem important," I said.

"And now it does?"

"Yeah, it fits with other things."

"What other things?" Hutt said. Klassen snorted. He couldn't hide his annoyance that I was being consulted.

"Maybe Andy had been passed over for the head greens keeper's job once too often," I said, "or he had some personal grudge against Harvey. I don't know, but it looks like he hung out at Riley's Rest for a few days. He worked out his plan, maybe screwed up his courage, and when he was ready, he arranged to meet Harvey. The wig fits in with his disguise as Wilma Taylor who is supposedly having an affair with Harvey. Andy's probably the one that tipped you off to the affair, eh. He shows up with the seven iron he took from Nick's bag and beats Harvey to death with it. He leaves the boat there and it floats away, ending up at Lasko Beach. He probably has some clothes hidden in the bush. He changes and heads up to the clubhouse where as casual as ever, he puts the bloodied club back in Nick's bag. The time fits too," I said, looking at Hutt. "Wilma's supposed to be on her way home from Prince Albert at the time of the murder."

"Who do you think killed Meyer, then?" Hutt asked me.

"I don't know," I said.

"Oh, you don't know?" Klassen sneered. "Well, maybe Nick Taylor shut him up because Andy knew he killed Kristoff. Taylor's the one with the motive. Here's Kristoff, who treated him like dog shit for years, gets him fired from his job, then has the balls to start porkin' his wife. That's one hell of a motive."

"It seems to me like somebody's trying to frame Nick?" I said

"What the hell are you talking about?" Klassen shouted.

Hutt turned a reproachful eye on him then asked me the question that must have been at the top of their list. "Do you know where Taylor is?"

I shook my head. "No, why should I?"

"Well you seem to know everything else," Klassen said.

"He's a fugitive from the law," Hutt said. "Should you refuse to divulge information about his whereabouts, you could be considered an accessory to murder."

"Oh," I said, feeling blood rush to my face.

"Think about it, pal," Klassen said as he ushered me out of the office.

Pulling into the Taylor's driveway, I saw Wilma in the back yard. She wore baggy sweat pants and was raking the lawn. Chipshot lay near by keeping an eye on things.

When she saw me she leaned the rake against the wheelbarrow.

"Hey Wilma, how're you doing?" I greeted her as I got out of the truck.

She just shook her head miserably.

"Come on, things aren't that bad," I said, giving her a squeeze around the shoulders. The dog whined consolingly. "But we've gotta get Nick back here as soon as possible. Where do you think he would go?" I asked.

"I don't know," she moaned.

"The longer he stays away the guiltier he looks," I said. "Even people who are on his side are losing faith."

Wilma looked a little lost. "I don't know where he is. I'd be the last person he'd tell," she said. "He thinks I'm a whore and a traitor." Chipshot trotted over and rubbed up against Wilma's legs.

"We need to find him," I said, "tell him to get his butt back here. Where would he go? Do you have any ideas at all?"

"Well," Wilma nudged a pile of grass clippings with her rubber boot, "maybe one."

With a six-pack of *Pil* beside me on the seat, I drove to a small town called Begins. Begins, its name not withstanding, is pretty much at the end of its days. A few people still live there, but mostly its just some abandoned buildings and a couple of old elevators eroding in the prairie wind.

Wilma had directed me to one of these elevators, said it was the only place she could think of where Nick might be hiding. "If he's still in these parts," she'd added. I parked in the shade, next to the loading ramp. Once inside I shouted Nick's name several times. There was no response.

A maintenance stairway led into the dark upper reaches of the building. I began the climb, a little uneasy and without much hope. Light leaked through cracks in the old structure where weather and age had pulled it apart. A layer of dust and chaff covered the stairway so I held on to the handrail as I climbed. As I neared the top I heard something other than my own creaking tread. It came from the broad shoulder of the building. I listened, breathing hard from the climb, then I called Nick's name.

When he finally answered, his voice was muted by the porous wood. "What the fuck are you doing here?"

"What the fuck are you doing here?" I said back, a little startled.

"What does it look like?" He emerged from the shadows, covered in dust, shafts of straw clinging to his unruly hair.

"You okay?" I said.

"I'm okay."

I remembered the six-pack down in the truck.

"How'd you find me?"

"Wilma figured you might be here." I looked around at the giant funnels, pulleys and partitions. "Why here?"

"We used to come up here and…you know." Nick made a rude gesture to indicate his meaning.

"Hiding out like this makes you look guilty, my friend. And it's not only the cops who think so. A lot of people are beginning to wonder." I didn't tell him that even his own kids were questioning his innocence.

"Crooked Lake and everybody in it can kiss my ass," Nick said, angrily, sending dust in every direction. Those people are only too happy to see me locked up. They already think I'm a thief; and now a murderer. A double murderer, a goddamned serial killer is what I am. Well fuck it, Bart. I've had it."

"Calm down," I said. "There are still people out there who believe in you," I said. "Don't forget about them."

Nick shook his head miserably, just as Wilma had.

"I believe in you," I said.

"That means a lot to me, Bart."

"Besides, I owe you." We'd never talked about that time on the lake, and by Nick's reaction we wouldn't now either; but it had always been there, buoying up our friendship, especially in times of trouble. "You can't stay here for ever, you know," I said.

"I can stay until the cops figure out who really killed those guys," he said.

"They're not going to do that," I said. "They think you're their guy. And if you're running, you must be guilty. Nick, why don't you just turn yourself in, it would make things a lot easier. For you, and your family."

He hesitated for a long moment, as though trying to make up his mind. Then he said, "I'm staying."

All of a sudden I felt unnerved in his presence. Maybe the words "accessory to murder" had something to do with it. "Okay, you take care," I said, reaching for the stair railing. "I want you to know I'm doing everything I can."

"I know," he said, nodding his head.

"There'll be a six-pack of Pilsner just inside the door," I said. Now the cops could add aiding and abetting to their list of charges against me.

14

When I got home, Rosie was on the phone. She mouthed Annie to me. "Don't cry. It'll be all right, honey. I know, I know. When? What did he say? Well, that's not such a bad thing. Annie, why don't you come home tonight?" Pause. "What time's your first class?" Pause. "Then come home and we'll have a nice supper and talk about it, okay?"

I waved to Rosie to let me speak to Annie. "Hi sweetheart." Sniffling over the line. "I hear you're coming home tonight?" Silence. "I'll make a special batch of Gran's Chicken Paprika, how does that sound? What time will you be home? Honey?"

A tear-choked response.

"Great, we'll see you then." I hung up.

"What the hell's going on?" I said to Rosie.

"Randall said he needed some space."

"What the hell's his problem?"

"Now don't start yelling."

"I'm not yelling," I yelled. "I just want to know what he's doing to my daughter."

"I don't know anymore than you do. We'll just have to wait until Annie gets here. But I'm warning you, Bart, don't you start in on her. She's upset enough without you making it worse."

"I don't want Annie hurt," I said, "that's all."

We had a late dinner, deciding on a clear soup and egg salad sandwiches in anticipation of the heavy supper to come. Forgoing my usual after dinner nap, I went to round up the ingredients for the Chicken Paprika.

I would need a nice fresh broiler, smoked bacon and some good paprika. There was an excellent butcher shop in Wallburg and since I had to look at some propane water heaters there anyway, I decided to drive the twenty or so kilometers south. It would give me a chance to test out my truck on the highway for the first time since *the accident*.

The little town of Wallburg squats along a curve on Highway Four. The curve carries on through most of the streets, giving the town a crescent shape, unique in the usual survey of square prairie towns. I steered the truck down Wally Drive, a pleasant poplar-lined gravel road that led into town. Turning left, I followed a curved street that took me to Strechuck's Plumbing and Heating.

There'd always been a friendly rivalry between Crooked Lake and Wallburg, and naturally that extended into the realm of hockey. Alistair Strechuck, better known as Stretch, was a rough and tumble defenseman who used intimidation to make up for what he lacked in ability. We'd played against each other in bantams, moved through midgets, then senior and now the rivalry continued in old-timers' hockey.

Stretch was a tall, lanky guy with a jutting jaw and a huge Adams apple. It bounced up and down freely as he greeted me. "Hey, how're things up in Little Chicago?"

I frowned.

"What the hell's goin' on up there anyway?" He aimed his angular chin in the direction of Crooked Lake.

"You got me," I said.

Stretch and Nick Taylor had had a not so friendly rivalry through their hockey careers. It was a lopsided match up. Nick at five foot eight, and Stretch nearly a foot taller. "Do you think Taylor killed those guys?" he asked.

"No, I don't."

"Cops have any other suspects?"

"They seem to be putting all their eggs in Nick's basket. Now, what about those heaters?"

After examining a variety of propane water heaters, their options and specs, I settled on two of them for my cabins at the lodge. I also got a couple of new propane bottles to replace ones that had expired, and the promise that Stretch would have everything waiting at the water base in La Ronge, ready to be flown up to Stuart Lake when we opened camp on June first.

"You know Meyer used to come into the pub here once in a while," Stretch said, as I was about to leave.

"He did, eh?"

"Yeah, played the VLTs mostly."

"Winning or losing?" I asked.

"There's no winning on those things."

"Did he drink much?"

"Not that you'd notice."

"Did he know anybody around here?"

"Didn't seem to. He came in with a woman once or twice."

"Know who she was?"

"No. The two of them seemed pretty cozy, though. Nice lookin' redhead."

Speculating on who the woman might be, I drove the few blocks over to the butcher shop to get my ingredients for supper. Ralph Nagy greeted me wearing a blood stained apron over his round middle. White haired and flushed as usual, Ralph stood behind his cooler which displayed an impressive array of beef, fresh poultry, bacon and a variety of sausages made by Ralph and his son Ralph Jr. He picked out a fine big bird and some double-smoked bacon along with an ounce of his best paprika, imported directly from Hungary. Ralph too brought up the Little Chicago epithet, which had been conferred upon Crooked Lake owing to a CBC television special.

Everyone was excited as big television vans rolled into town that summer and household names strolled up and down the streets. Television crews were all over, ostensibly filming Crooked Lake's seventy-fifth anniversary celebrations.

But the people were shocked when the program aired. It wasn't about Crooked Lake's homecoming celebrations at all. Instead, it sensationalized what it called the town's sordid past, documenting a time when it had the only RCMP detachment for hundreds of square miles. Every crime that was committed in the vast area was reported to the Crooked Lake detachment, hence the town's infamous reputation.

Dee Elliot's dad had been interviewed and had extolled the virtues of Crooked Lake, only to be disgusted by the way a trusted institution like the CBC could twist his words to support the ill-conceived contentions of the producers. Though now it would seem those contentions were becoming more of a reality than ever.

Hauling my six-foot-one-inch frame into my pick-up, I realized that for the first day since being pushed into that ravine, I felt no discernible pain or discomfort. The headaches had ceased a few days earlier and a visit with our chiropractor had put my neck back in place. People had even stopped commenting on my battered face, although sidelong glances did indicate I wasn't completely healed. As my truck purred along at about sixty, acting like a young stud, I thought about Andy Meyer and the mystery lady who sat cozily next to him playing VLTs in the Wallburg Hotel.

Like Lloyd Hughes said, Andy wasn't the type of guy to attract a lot of friends, much less a female friend. 'Course they say every man has his mate and maybe Andy had found his. As I tried to remember the old song that expressed that sentiment, I noticed a red light flashing in my rear-view mirror. Instinctively, I looked down at my speedometer. Damn. I was surprised to see I had crept up to seventy-five miles per hour.

After I'd pulled on to the shoulder, Corporal Fred Snell pulled in behind me and got out of the police cruiser. Walking up to my window, he said, "Going a little fast aren't you, Bart?"

"I guess Ernie has this thing running even better than I thought," I said.

I opened the door and put a foot on the running board, half expecting Fred to start writing up a ticket, but instead he said, "We just got the results back on Meyer's autopsy."

Hopping down, I leaned against my new paint job and crossed my arms as if to say it made no difference to me.

Fred took on a confidential tone. "Turns out it wasn't the injury to his head that killed him."

My indifference gone, I said, "What the hell did kill him then?"

"Poison."

"Poison?" Having seen Andy on the floor of that trailer, it was inconceivable that he'd been killed by anything other than… "You're telling me that Andy was poisoned? What, *then* somebody bashed him over the head?"

"Looks like it."

"Jesus Christ. What was it?"

"What?"

"The poison."

He shook his head. "We don't have all the results yet. The pathologist thinks Andy may have ingested some kind of psychotropic drug, possibly LSD, and it was laced with something deadly."

I was surprised by his candor. "Why are you telling me all this, Fred?"

He hesitated for a moment, looking out over the gently rolling prairie. "Because I don't like what's going on. Hutt and Klassen, Crown counsel, the media, even some of our own detachment, all of them have their sights set on Nick. I don't know whether he's guilty or not, but damn it, I think we have to consider all the possibilities."

"Well, I'm glad somebody 's doing that," I said.

He shrugged and walked back to the cruiser. "Keep this under your hat, eh. And you didn't hear it from me."

After he had disappeared down the highway, I realized he'd pulled me over on Norman's Curve. Norman's Curve, where my dad had been killed in a head on collision when I was five years old. The accident had left my mother a broken woman and me a ward of my grandmother for several years. I kept it down to fifty-five for the remainder of my trip back to Crooked Lake.

I pulled into our driveway and was glad to see Annie's old Toyota parked behind Rosie's van. Inside, I placed my packages on the counter and found the two of them sitting in the living room. "Hey, there's my favourite daughter." I pulled Annie to her feet and gave her a hug. She trembled in my arms, and behind her I saw dismay on Rosie's face. "Everything's fine now," I said, "you're home." I smiled at her, but neither her mouth, nor her red-rimmed eyes smiled back.

A look from Rosie suggested I wasn't needed at the moment, so I went into the kitchen and put on my apron and the chef's hat the kids had given me for Christmas. I floured and seasoned the chicken that I'd cut into large meaty pieces, then fried onions and smoked bacon. While I worked, I tried, without much success, to pick up the murmured conversation between Rosie and Annie. I had managed to beg a quart of whole cream from a dairy farmer who lives on the edge of town. I would add that just before serving. As the chicken browned on the stovetop, I began mixing dough.

"Hey, you two," I called, "come out here, I need some help with these dumplings." I could make drop dumplings, but Rosie made them look so much better, forming them into little egg shapes.

A few minutes later, a gloomy Rosie walked into the kitchen. "What's going on?" I whispered. But before she could answer, an equally glum Annie came in and stood at the kitchen table. "So how about some help here, Annie?" I said in my most cheerful voice.

In response, she burst into tears and ran from the room.

"What the hell's going on?" I said to a pale Rosie. "Things can't be that bad, can they?"

"She's pregnant."

The Mack truck you always hear about hit me right about then. My Annie? My little girl? Pregnant? It couldn't be. What about all our plans, her plans, her future?

"Rosie," I cried, "tell me it's not true." Calamity ricocheted around my brain like a bullet.

Ever practical, Rosie raised her eyebrows, expressing at once that it was true, so let's cut the hysterics and figure out how to deal with it.

"Where the hell's Randall?" I said.

"He's at his folks in Moose Jaw. Says he needs some time to think."

"What's to think about?" Then a disturbing thought struck me. "It is his, isn't it?"

"Of course," Rosie scolded.

"What's to think about then?"

Again Rosie's eyebrows did the talking.

At least Stuart enjoyed the Chicken Paprika; the rest of us were too overwhelmed with our own thoughts to think about food, even extraordinary food. After pushing her meal around in her plate during supper, Annie went to her room, and wasn't heard from again.

Stuart was off to cadets complaining that his uniform was too tight around the middle. "I wish you wouldn't make such a good supper just before cadets," he said, "and everybody left the drumsticks for me."

Rosie and I cleared the table, stacking the dishes in the dishwasher. We sat close to each other on the couch, setting aside our differences for Annie's sake.

"I was so looking forward to her wedding," Rosie said. "Now there probably won't even be a wedding."

"There damn well better be a wedding," I said. But when tears began creeping down Rosie's cheeks, I said more gently, "Let's not get ahead of ourselves. They've been pretty happy together. And he's not a bad sort." Then I remembered the environmental study. "Will he still be coming up to the lodge?"

"I don't know," Rosie grumbled, clearly unhappy that I would be thinking about my own problems when our daughter was in trouble.

In trouble. I remembered the term from the old days. Usually only girls from the wrong side of the tracks got in trouble. And the consequences were often disastrous, from botched abortions to abandoned children. But that was one memory I didn't need rattling around in my brain right then.

"All I know," Rosie continued, "is that our daughter's future, her chance for a happy life is at stake. Damn, why did this have to happen? She was doing so well."

"Is she sure?" I asked.

"She got confirmation from the doctor this morning. She's in her sixth week."

"Didn't they use…" Rosie understood contraception by the inept look on my face.

"I guess so, but nothing's foolproof."

Later, lying in bed, we talked some more, agreeing that the important thing was to support Annie in every way we could. Maybe it was the stirring of deep emotions or our need for reassurance, but in the darkened room, Rosie and I made love with more passion than we had mustered in a long time.

Having breakfasted, we waited impatiently for Annie to get up. At ten o'clock, when we still hadn't heard a peep, Rosie and I set out on our daily walk. It was none too soon for Butch, who had grown accustomed to an early romp.

At noon Stuart stormed in, hungry as a bear. "Where's Annie?" he said.

I nodded toward her bedroom.

"Where's her car, then?"

"What?" Rosie said, confused.

"She must have left while we were out," I said. I felt a stab of guilt, I hadn't even gone in to say goodnight. Too busy satisfying my own needs. "How could she leave without a bloody word?" I said.

Rosie was already dialing Annie's number in the city. After several rings, she hung up. "No answer."

"What now?" I said.

"What's going on?" Stuart asked.

"We could try her at Randall's."

"I thought he was in Moose Jaw."

"What's going on?" Stuart asked again, but this time his mouth was full of leftover Chicken Paprika.

"Nothing dear, just eat your dinner," Rosie said, ladling a plateful for me.

We agreed to wait until suppertime to try Annie again. She was a levelheaded girl and we were sure she wouldn't do anything desperate. But that didn't make the waiting any easier.

In need of something to occupy my mind until suppertime, I decided to run into P.A. and talk to Nick's lawyer. I'd called the day before at the behest of Wilma Taylor. "I can't make head or tail of what's going on," she'd said. Apparently Frank Hendrickson's legalese was more than Wilma could handle.

We finished dinner with no further discussion about Annie; in fact, Stuart held forth with a diatribe about his commanding officer and how if this were the real military he'd probably be stripped of his rank for behavior unbefitting an officer, or maybe even court marshaled for endangering the lives of his men. You have to remember that Stuart has a lively imagination and took air cadets very seriously.

"Nobody listens to him anymore," Stuart said. "Mostly it's because he doesn't seem to care about the troop. He makes me do most of the drill work." Stuart had recently been promoted to the rank of sergeant. "And I'm beginning to think I know more than he does about airplanes, especially *WW II* planes."

"Discipline is the hallmark of a good soldier," I said. "That means following orders, not questioning superior officers or their motives. As second in command, Stuart, you should be supporting Captain Jarvis, setting an example for the rest of the troop. Let them know you're behind him a hundred percent."

"Your father's right, dear." Looking at her watch, Rosie added, "It's time for school."

Before rushing out, Stuart inhaled a piece of the chocolate pie that had gone largely untouched at last night's supper. Just before closing the door on his way out, he said, "He always smells like booze, too."

I showered, put on a fresh golf shirt and some new Dockers and started out for Prince Albert. The drive roams through rolling farmland that is dotted with sloughs and bush. Crossing the South Saskatchewan River, trees populate the landscape, and the forest, like a promise fulfilled, begins in earnest.

Frank Hendrickson had agreed to see me for a few minutes around three that afternoon. Having about forty-five minutes to kill, I stopped in at Wadner's. The new season's fresh supply of lures had me concentrating so hard that until he whacked me on the back, scaring the hell out of me, I hadn't noticed Gerald T. Meyer.

"Caught you, didn't I?" he said with a wheezy laugh.

"Yeah, I guess you did," I said, trying to regain my composure. "What are you doing here?"

"Well, even down in the bald prairie, we got some fishin' lakes. 'Course we don't got stores as good as this for tackle and such." It seemed that Gerald liked to play the good ol' boy.

I thought it was quite a coincidence, both of us showing up at Wadner's at the same time, but I didn't say so.

"What kind of fish do you catch down there?" I asked.

"Oh, a few suckers," he grinned, continuing his routine.

"You ever fished Last Mountain?"

"Hooked some good-sized trout there a few years ago," he boasted. "So, what are you buying?"

"Oh nothing much, just killing some time," I said, ignoring the dozen or so lures I held in my hand.

"Waitin' for something, are you?"

"Not really," I said defensively. For some reason, the guy was giving me the creeps. Maybe it was the way he looked at me, or didn't look at me. I dumped the lures back on the shelf in a heap.

"Can I ask you a question?" Gerald said.

"Sure," I said.

He looked up and down the aisle before saying in an undertone, "Was my brother still alive when you found him?"

"No," I said, surprised by the question. "At least, as far as I could tell he wasn't."

"He didn't say anything then?"

"No."

"Nothing at all?"

"No."

"You sure?"

"Yes, I'm sure. He was just lying there, dead, you know?."

"Hey, don't go gettin' your shit in a knot, eh." He grinned broadley. "Catch you back in Crooked Lake."

"What?" I said, puzzled for a moment. "Oh, yeah."

The grin remained on his grizzled face, but his eyes had turned cold.

Outside of Wadner's, I glanced up and down the block, but didn't spot Gerald's four-by-four. I pondered what it was that was bothering me about Gerald. In Crooked Lake he'd been just a red-necked ruffian, but now he seemed devious, even menacing. And what was he doing here? He was certainly no fisherman. I knew for a fact there were no trout in Last Mountain Lake.

Hendrickson's cover-girl receptionist ushered me into the attorney's office.

"What can I do for you?" he said. "As I told you on the phone, I don't have a lot of time." A golf club lay across his desk.

"Wilma asked me to see you. She's a little frustrated, feels you haven't filled her in on what's happening."

"I've spoken to her a number of times. I thought I had been clear enough," he said. "I don't know what else there is I can tell her, but I could give her another call."

"Maybe if you just explain it to me," I said, "I can pass it on. Perhaps in a way that she can understand," I added slowly and precisely.

"Well, there isn't a hell of a whole lot to tell," he said, obviously not wanting to discuss the matter at length. "Until Nick turns himself in or is apprehended, there's not much I can do."

"You can do what it takes to prove he's innocent," I said, giving Hendrickson my meaningful look.

He fingered the shaft of his golf club. "I didn't want to tell Wilma straight out," he said, "but when the time comes, I'll recommend that Nick take a plea."

"A plea?"

"Yes."

"What exactly does that mean?" I asked.

"In exchange for a guilty plea, we get a reduced charge and with it a reduced sentence. Perhaps manslaughter in the death of Kristoff. We would argue act of passion in light of the affair. And maybe we can bargain down from first degree in Meyer's case."

"Don't you have to talk to Nick, get his side of the story?"

"There's nothing I'd like better," he said.

"Well, don't jump the gun, eh. The police have no real proof, just a lot of circumstantial evidence. And are you aware," I said, "that Andy Meyer did not die from a blow to the head?"

"No?" Hendrickson said, a mixture of alarm and amusement in his eyes.

"No," I said, "he was poisoned."

Hendrickson thought about it for a moment, then said, "And this fact comes from?"

"Let's just say a very reliable source."

I could almost hear the lawyer's brain churning out his options. Finally, he chose to accept an awkward situation for what it was. "Should that source be correct," he said, "it would put a slightly different slant on things." He pressed a button on his phone. "Janice, could you bring in some coffee and would you call the club and put off my tee time until later."

"What time?" Miss Chatelaine asked.

"I don't know, whatever's available," he said, clearly disappointed his golf game had to be postponed. He then put in a call to the Crown prosecutor in Saskatoon who confirmed the cause of death and cautioned Hendrickson that it was to be kept confidential, as police were still following up leads. Hendrickson complained that the vital information should have come through official channels and not through, what he called, the rumour mill.

With steaming cups of coffee, cream and sugar and what looked like homemade cookies sitting in front of us, the lawyer said, "The cause of death certainly brings up a few questions."

"I really can't see Nick poisoning anybody," I said.

He offered me a cookie; they weren't homemade, but tasty, nonetheless.

"So what's next?" I asked.

"First of all, do you have any idea where he is?"

I was tempted to tell him about the abandoned elevator in Begins, but because I knew Nick would never forgive me, I said, "None."

Hendrickson didn't look entirely convinced. "This disappearing act certainly doesn't help Nick's case," he said.

"I know. But why would Nick kill Andy Meyer?"

"Well," Hendrickson said, "the police think he did it to keep Meyer from testifying in Kristoff's murder."

"But, if Andy knew something about Harvey's murder, wouldn't he have come forward with it before? And what about the wig?"

"What wig?"

"You don't know about the wig, either?" I said. "You're Nick's lawyer for God sake, you're supposed to know about these things. Anyway, I saw a wig at Riley's cottage. And the police found one at Andy's trailer."

"So?" Hendrickson said.

I was a little troubled by his attitude. "It makes you wonder; was it the same wig, and why would he have a wig?"

"Yes?"

"Well, you're the lawyer." When he didn't respond, I said, "I think Andy used the wig as part of his disguise." Hendrickson stared at me blankly, so I went on to describe what I'd told the police.

By the time we were done, we'd polished off the cookies, and the lawyer was convinced that Nick might have a better chance than he had first thought. Now if only Nick would turn himself in.

15

It was suppertime when I reached the edge of the Potato River Valley and followed the gently winding road into Crooked Lake. Glowering thunderheads were piled up to the south, but the valley, kissed by the sun, remained as serene as ever.

We sat down to a hearty meal of thick soup with good wholegrain bread, willing ourselves to wait until after supper before calling Annie. Just as I was refilling my bowl, the phone rang. I picked up.

"Dad," Annie's voice was faint.

"Annie," I said looking at Rosie. "Are you all right?"

"I'm fine, Dad. Sorry I took off like that."

"It's okay, honey. It's just we were worried."

There were a few moments of silence on the line, then Annie sobbed, "Oh, Daddy..."

"It's okay, sweetheart." I could almost hear the tears trickle down her cheeks. "We can be there in an hour, you don't have to go through this by your self."

"No," she said forcefully. "I need to be on my own right now. And...I made an appointment to see a counselor tomorrow."

"What kind of counselor?"

"Counselor?" Rosie said.

"Someone who has some experience with," she hesitated, "this sort of thing."

"Honey, your mother and I have some experience with this sort of thing."

"I know, Dad. I just want to, you know, talk to somebody who's...objective, and she's a trained psychologist too."

"Well, if that's what you want."

"Dad," she said almost apologetically, "could I talk to Mom for a sec?"

"Sure, honey."

"Dad," she said, "I love you."

"I love you too, Annie."

I assumed, perhaps naively, that counselors were only for sick people. Rosie and I were still of the *rely-on-you-and-yours* mode of thinking, I guess.

After Rosie hung up, I said, "She's a mature young woman, she'll assess things and make up her mind after she's seen this counselor. That's wise, right?"

"I guess so." Rosie seemed unconvinced.

"What about Randall?" I asked.

"Well, she's not very happy he took off. But she loves him," Rosie said, "I know she does."

Thunder grumbled nearby as we sat in silence speculating on what lay ahead.

"Maybe I should call Randall," I said.

"Don't you dare! That's all she needs." Rosie took a deep breath, exhaling slowly. "Let's just let her do things her way and see what happens."

As we sat at the kitchen table, a flash of lightning illuminated the crescent. I had a fleeting image of Gerald T.'s four-by-four. I wasn't sure if it was real or if I'd only imagined it. The peculiar feeling I'd had that morning returned and I wondered if Gerald's presence at Wadner's had simply been coincidence or something more sinister.

Feeling a bit dogged after a restless night's sleep, I found Rosie in the kitchen, baking. I poured myself a cup of coffee and watched as she smeared copious amounts of butter over a large rectangle of neatly flattened dough. She applied a layer of rich brown sugar, scattered raisins and a few walnuts over it and finally dusted the whole thing generously with cinnamon.

I set off for the post office, my taste buds firing in anticipation of Rosie's fresh baked cinnamon rolls. I parked in front of a brand new mini-van.

Lloyd Hughes got out of the van and stepped up to my door. "I wanted to let you know," he said, "we've got a board meeting set up for next week. We've got to think about replacing Harvey, and now there's Andy."

It was true, we'd lost both a board member and now our assistant greens keeper. With everything that was going on, I'd all but forgotten how the golf course was managing.

"With all the work out there," Lloyd said, squinting against the shine of my new paint job, "we need to get Ron Diccum some help."

"Let's make it a local person," I said, "and Lloyd, don't count out women this time." He and Harvey had invariably spoken against women applicants.

"Sure, Bart," he said halfheartedly.

After cleaning out my mailbox and being told about the meeting again by Les Thatcher, I crossed the street to *the Reporter*. "I wonder if you could do me a favour?" I asked Dee Elliot. "I'd like to get the scoop on Gerald Meyer."

"Andy's brother?"

"Yeah, I want to see what kind of reputation he's got down in Zenita. He claims to be some kind of tough guy. Maybe you can find out if he's got a criminal record."

Dee raised her eyebrows. "What's this all about?"

"Nothing." After all, it was entirely possible that Gerald was looking for fishing tackle; and that I didn't see his truck drive by my house last night.

"It must be something," she insisted.

"I'd just like to know a little more about him, that's all," I said.

"Okay," she said, a little exasperated, "I'll see what I can do."

"And Dee, Gerald T. is not a friendly giant, so be discreet."

"Gotcha." She gave me an exaggerated wink.

From *the Reporter* I drove over to Nick and Wilma's house. I knew Wilma would want an account of my visit with Hendrickson.

Having been on leave from her job, Wilma planned to return to work the following Monday. "I just can't sit around any more. I'm going stir crazy, and besides the kids act like they don't need me, and with Nick..." she faltered, a lump in her throat. "Was he there?"

I shook my head. "No." I figured it would serve no purpose to tell her Nick was hiding in their old love nest. Nor did she need to be part of the cover-up.

We settled in the living room. "So, what did Hendrickson say?" she asked in a tone that suggested she didn't expect much.

I didn't want to get her hopes up, but at the same time I did want to leave her with some. "He thinks the case against Nick for Andy's murder is pretty thin. And if he can disprove that, he feels it will weaken the case against him for Harvey's."

"Really?" Her voice yearned for reassurance.

I went on to describe the hour-long discussion that I'd had with Hendrickson. I tried to keep it upbeat, but mentioned the plea-bargain at the end just to be accurate.

"Do you really think things could be back to normal?" Wilma said. "If only I could talk to Nick, tell him." I noticed dark rings under Wilma's amber eyes. "You never know how good you've got it, until something like this happens," she said. Normally an outgoing person, Wilma now avoided her regular haunts and spent most of her time at home overwhelming her kids with attention.

"There's no guarantee of course," I said. "The Crown still wants Nick for two murders." Her face fell. "It's a matter of establishing doubt in the mind of the jury, and Hendrickson thinks…thinks," I emphasized, "that he can do that. But, Nick has to give himself up before any of this can happen. Another thing," I said. "I don't know about Hendrickson. I'm not sure if he's got what it takes."

"He did okay at the preliminary," Wilma said.

"True, but you really didn't hire him to defend Nick for murder."

"I know, and he's costing us a fortune too. We gave him a seventy-five hundred dollar retainer and he says that's just to start."

"What about another lawyer?"

"We talked about it, but..."

"They say the best in the province for this kind of thing is Harold Kline. Maybe Nick would come in if he knew he had a good lawyer. 'Course Kline would definitely cost you more, eh."

"What a rotten system," Wilma said. "The police charge you on the flimsiest evidence, and you end up going broke defending yourself. Goddamnit. How are we going to get through this? We already took the equity out of the house to pay Nick's bail. Now we're living off our credit cards."

Both Nick and Wilma had worked hard all their lives, Wilma for SaslTel, and Nick taking what he could get in addition to his greens keeping job. In the winter he ran the Zamboni at the skating rink or stood guard at the jail. But with everyday expenses and trying to provide the best for their kids, they usually had little left at the end of the month.

The marriage too was under great strain what with Wilma's alleged libidinous indiscretions. Nor did it help that the two of them were the object of the juiciest gossip the town had heard for a long time.

Devouring my second warm cinnamon roll, I said to Rosie, "I wish there was some way to help Nick and Wilma with their legal costs."

Rosie looked thoughtful. I eyed a third bun.

When I awoke from my pastry-addled nap, Rosie was in the middle of organizing a fundraiser. By that night the Old Timers' Hockey Association, with Rosie as Secretary Treasurer, had planned a casino to be held at the Rec Centre.

"People love to gamble," Rosie said, "especially for a good cause."

"You're just like the government."

Ignoring me, she went on, "We've got Carlton's Casino coming. They'll bring all the equipment along with operators and dealers." She checked off items on her list. "There'll be lucky seven, blackjack, crown and anchor, we'll have bingo, bowling for dollars; and the players' wives have volunteered to run the concession." An ad was squeezed into *the Reporter* well after deadline and Dee Elliot agreed to put together a poster for the event, gratis.

I spent a couple of hours in the bear pit firming up reservations with travel agents and responding to messages left on our eight hundred line. The lodge was booked for the season that runs from just after the ice breaks up at the end of May until the Thanksgiving Day weekend.

When I was done with my paperwork, I sat there browsing the framed photographs that hang randomly on the walls of my office. Pictures taken over the years, depicting the evolution of the lodge and our family. Me, standing on the float of a leased Cessna 185. I had just landed in the bay that would one day become home to Stuart Lake Lodge. Then there was Rosie catching her first trout, a nice six-pounder, and next to that, four year old Annie helping our guide, Charlie Mackenzie, fry the fish over an open fire.

After getting a pilot's license, I dreamed of becoming a bush pilot. But after a summer as a wingman for a small floatplane outfit in northern Manitoba, I realized I didn't like commercial flying all that much.

But I did love the north, and I enjoyed landing at remote fishing lodges, and meeting the outfitters. Like the crusty old bushman who kept a pet black bear. The damn thing got into the plane one time and nearly chewed the leg off one of our passengers. Then there was the friendly Quebecois couple who fed us beans and bacon swimming in maple syrup every time we landed at their remote lodge. They always had a big Canadian flag flying.

Despite their eccentricities, or maybe because of them, these people had a real passion for the wilderness. That summer, at twenty-three, I realized I too had that passion, and decided to build my own lodge.

I soon ran into my first big hurdle, the fathomless depths of government bureaucracy. After six months of meetings with civil servants, and an endless number of trips to government offices, I seemed no closer to getting the lease than the day I had first landed on Stuart Lake.

It wasn't until I contacted our MLA, Ben Stonechild, that things began to progress. Ben was just as outraged as I that the process had taken so long and was anxious to provide jobs for the unemployed in the area. Even with his help, it took another several months, but finally the renewable fifteen-year lease had been granted.

Recently the increase in the value of gold and the discovery of huge diamond reserves has led to a frenzy of companies exploring northern Saskatchewan. The government has been flooded with applications to develop claims. We'd built up a thriving business over the years, but we could lose it all if we don't get that lease renewed.

The phone rang, jarring me from my reverie. Could we squeeze in one more party before freeze up in the fall? Maybe.

16

When *the Reporter* hit the streets that Thursday morning, it wasn't the front page or even *local and general* news that had everyone buzzing; it was a curt, anonymous letter to the editor.

To the citizens of Crooked Lake:
It's no secret to Him that behind your mask of propriety lurks a town filled with lies, disguise and betrayal. Murder, good citizens, is symptomatic of moral bankruptcy. The Lord will be my judge and confessor and I will pay for my sins when I stand before Him, but so too will you.

That morning coffee row had expanded, with clutches of discussion groups well beyond the counter, to booths and tables. When I walked into the Junction Stop with Rosie, eyes turned our way and the roar dwindled to a low purr. Apparently my discreet inquiries had become more public than I had realized.

"Morning, Bart," said the ever-present Bill Bird. "Seen the paper?"

I held up the copy I was carrying.

"So, what do you think," he said, as though he were addressing a group of students, "is that a letter from the murderer?"

Now all eyes were trained on me, including Rosie's. "To me it looks like the ravings of some religious fanatic," I replied.

"Yes, but he says," and here the teacher professorially put on his glasses and read, "the Lord will be my judge and confessor and I will pay for my sins when I stand before him."

"Isn't that true of us all?" I replied.

"He's blaming the whole town," put in the gas jockey, "like Crooked Lake is some kinda sin bin, or something, eh."

"It could be this person is not all there," I said.

"You mean he's nuts?" said the gas jockey.

"Or maybe just sniffed a little too much gas," somebody threw in from one of the booths, getting a chuckle from the gathering.

"What makes you so sure the murderer is a he?" Rosie said.

Coffee Row was struck dumb for a few moments, until Lefty Holdner broke the silence. "There's no woman strong enough to do in two men like that, eh. It takes a lot to crack a guy's skull."

An uncomfortable quiet engulfed the restaurant followed by a mumbling shuffle, as people discussed the possibilities, ordered more coffee or headed back to work.

"Do you think it was a woman?" Ernie Haidu asked as he and Lefty got up to return to the Esso Station.

"Why not?" Rosie responded offhandedly. Lefty shook his head. Rosie had made no comment on the murders before this. I assumed she had no opinions on the matter, but maybe I was wrong. Perhaps she just didn't want to encourage me.

"So," I said as we drove home, "what makes you think it was a woman?"

"Poison." I'd passed on Fred Snell's roadside report. "It's a woman's means of offing somebody, eh," she said. "A man shoots, stabs, strangles and bashes people over the head. A woman simply slips something into their drink. A much less messy way to go." I couldn't argue with her logic.

"But what about the skull-cracking?"

"Well, the woman, who must have been a friend or certainly an acquaintance, probably slipped something into Andy's drink or food or whatever, expecting him to quietly go to sleep and simply not wake up again. But, shortly after that Nick comes along and she's forced to brain Andy before the poison has had a chance to do its job."

"You think?"

"Well, what other explanation could there be?"

What indeed?

I dropped Rosie off at home and went to have a little chat with Stuart's cadet leader, Gilbert Jarvis. As secretary-treasurer of the R.M. of Crooked Lake, he was in charge of a rural municipality that had once been populated by hundreds of farmers and their families. The transformation to mega farming had reduced the R.M. to less than a hundred farmers, many of who lived in town and for that reason were known as sidewalk farmers.

The R.M. office, a fifties, wood-frame building stood next to the liquor store on Main Street. When I opened the heavy metal door, it squealed like a pig. "You oughta put some oil on that, Gil," I said.

"Yeah, I been meaning to," he said, setting down his coffee cup among piles of papers and stacks of file folders on his cluttered desktop.

"Looks like you're keeping busy," I said.

"Yeah, since I was forced to let Eleanor go, the work is really piling up."

"That must have been quite a blow to poor Eleanor."

He nodded in assent. "She's been coming around a lot since. Asking if there's been any change, as if all of a sudden the family farm is going to make a comeback."

"Must be hell to lose your job like that." I thought about how Nick was handling it, and then how I might.

"A couple of days ago," he said, "she hung around out front for practically the whole afternoon. Personally," he said, a slight slur in his speech, "I think she needs help."

We shook our heads in a regretful manner, neither of us willing to speculate on what kind of help. I wondered if it was Eleanor who'd written the letter to the editor.

The old floorboards creaked under my feet. "Taxes going up again this year?" I asked.

"I think the mill rate will be stable, but that's only a guess," Gil said. Crooked Lake—the lake—fell under the jurisdiction of the R.M. of St. Hubert and the cost of adding infrastructure recently had resulted in tax hikes for each of the past three years. "Depends on the number of development permits that are approved."

"I thought development had been frozen." Surrounded by close to a thousand cottages, there was a real concern for the lake's sustainability.

"It has," Gil said, "except for a few properties, the biggest chunk being two quarters of land north of Grayham Point. They fall under the old regulations."

The freeze was a contentious issue. Many property owners had been left high and dry because of it.

I noticed Gil had carefully pushed his cup further behind a tall stack of manila folders. "The two quarters had been approved just before the freeze came into effect. So, by rights the land is still eligible for development."

"Who owns this land?" I asked.

"We have confidentiality rules," he answered.

"I understand," I said.

"But," Gil seemed ready to talk, "since the owner is deceased, it's probably okay."

"Deceased?"

"Yeah," Gil said. "It was Harvey Kristoff's land."

"Harvey? I wonder why he didn't develop it?"

"Probably waiting for demand to increase. Prices have been going up steadily since the freeze. Harvey was a savvy businessman. In fact he had come in to pick up an application form just before..."

"Development application?"

"Of sorts. Apparently he was about to gift the land to someone, but in order to grandfather the development rights, he had to apply to transfer the permit."

"Who was he gifting the land to?"

"I don't know. He never brought the application back."

I was surprised at Harvey's generosity. It didn't jibe with what I knew of him. But I hadn't come to discuss Harvey.

"So, how're cadets going?" I said.

"Fine." A not very convincing smile slid across Gil's face.

"I know Stuart appreciates everything you've done. He'd never have made sergeant at his age without your guidance and support."

"Well, I do what I can." Gil's eyes wondered over to his cup.

"But there's something that concerns me," I said.

He looked back at me warily.

"I think you know what it is."

"What?" he said, looking away.

"It's the drinking, Gil."

It looked like he might try to deny it, but the protest died on his lips. He sat back limply in his chair and stared at a small empty spot on his desk.

"Those kids are smart," I said, "and in some ways ruthless. The respect that takes so long to build can be lost very quickly and I'm afraid that's what's happening." I leaned an elbow on the counter. "You know Gil, what you do at home or for that matter here in your office," I nodded towards the cup behind the pile of folders, "is your business. But what you do when you have the welfare of children in your hands, and in particular my child, is a different thing. Then it becomes my business."

He covered his face with his hands as if to rub away reality. I was reminded of Nick doing the same thing.

"Can you stop drinking?" I asked.

As if in anticipation of being sober, he shuddered. "I can try."

"That's not good enough, Gil. Those kids deserve better. They've put their faith in you and so have their parents."

Gil sat there, saying nothing. In the silence, an image of my mother came to me. She no longer cooked or cleaned the house. She just sat day after day and stared through the window, looking out on the abandoned garden. I remembered Gran coming to the house, washing clothes and giving me a bath while Uncle Rudy cut the grass and fixed my wagon. Then one day they packed up all my things in two big boxes. All my toys. We drove the dusty road to Gran's farm. I didn't see Mom after that. Not for a long time.

The kids used to tease me when I started school. *North Battleford.* They'd use the name like a stick. I didn't know what it meant until later, when I learned they were referring to the mental hospital in North Battleford where my mother had been sent.

It was my birthday and I was keenly awaiting Dad's return from the city. He never did return. It was a head-on collision just a few miles south of Crooked Lake, at Norman's Curve. Witnesses at the inquest said the man driving the other car had spent most of the afternoon drinking in the pub. At just five years of age, I didn't understand, but I guess Mom went around the bend that day, and my birthday present got all smashed up.

I found myself getting angry. "Goddamnit, Gil."

"Joan left me," he said, barely audible. "I just haven't been able to face it... I don't know what to do."

We were silent for several moments. Two men grieving the misfortunes of life.

"Nobody knows yet," he said, an entreaty to be discreet. "We haven't even told our kids." He took a deep breath. "I'm sorry about the cadets, Bart."

"I'm sorry too," I said.

I left him slouched behind his cluttered desk, his eyes staring at the empty spot on its surface.

17

Kristoff's lake front property had been neglected. The grass needed cutting, the windbreak of poplars was dotted with dandelions and the garden, unlike my own, hosted a variety of weeds. Harvey's forest green SUV was parked in front of the garage and the sun glinted off the burgundy hood of a new Oldsmobile that sat next to the house.

I was curious about the two quarters of land that Gil had told me about and reasoned that sufficient time had elapsed to visit Harvey's aggrieved widow. A friendly-looking schnauzer met me as I pulled into the yard. After a few greeting barks, he trotted over to my truck and waited for me to get out. Inside the house, I saw a curtain move. A few moments later the door swung open and Ellen Kristoff emerged, shading her eyes from the noonday sun, a bemused look on her face.

"Good morning, Ellen," I said, approaching the house while the schnauzer did his best to impede my progress.

"Morning," she said, crossing the covered veranda that surrounded three sides of the rambling one story house. Ellen Kristoff was an attractive woman. She had medium length graying hair pulled back in a ponytail and deep-set, soulful eyes. She wore no make-up and was nicely squeezed into some sort of exercise outfit. As I got up close, the lines on her face suggested a weariness for which I could not blame her.

I gave her my meaningful look and asked in sympathetic tones, "How're you holding up?"

"Fine, thank you." We didn't know each other well, but in a town the size of Crooked Lake you got to know most everyone. "Won't you come in?" she said. There were serving platters, casserole dishes and salad bowls, washed and piled up on the counter. They were, no doubt, waiting to be returned to the generous folks who had, following tradition, sent food to the bereaved.

"Can I get you a cup of coffee?" She motioned for me to proceed into the living room. It was large though sparsely furnished, with an expansive view of the bay through giant floor-to-ceiling windows. I remembered Rosie gushing over the Kristoff house when it was built. Prairie Modern, she called it. She'd read about the Erickson-influenced architectural style in *Saskatchewan Magazine*.

"Thanks," I said, taking a seat on a leather couch that sat across from a matching lazy boy. The chair was pointed at a big-screen TV. A grand piano looked ignored on the far side of the room. Opposite the couch was a bar, replete with sink, fridge and overhead racks suspending all manner of glasses. As I made myself comfortable in the buttery leather couch, I perused the contents of a small bookcase; it contained mainly hardcover tomes with names I didn't recognize interspersed with the odd thriller, and of course, the requisite Bible, a well worn leather-bound edition. A few minutes later Ellen carried in a tray with coffee, cream and sugar.

"How's Rosie?" she asked, setting the tray on the coffee table. She took a seat at the other end of the nine-foot couch.

"Oh, she's fine," I said, "keeping busy." I had to bite my tongue about the casino. I wanted to talk about the two quarters of land, but instead, I said, "I just wanted to come by and say hello. See if there's anything we can do. Noticed your grass needs cutting."

"I have someone coming by later today actually," she said, "and I plan to get to the weeding too. My garden's in a state. I haven't been in it since the day Harvey was..." She bowed her head and brought her hands together on her lap. "I love to garden," she said, and smiled as if to ward off falling victim to her emotions. "By the way, I was sorry to hear about your accident," she said.

I nodded in acknowledgement, and once again fought the urge to contradict the *accident* report.

"Are you all right?" she asked. "You were lucky to survive, I understand."

"Well, I did take a few bumps, but Doc Chow put me back on my feet pretty quick."

She nodded her head demurely, "I'm glad," she said then seemed content to sit and look out over the water.

"Ellen, I was wondering if you had any thoughts on the who or why of it?"

I didn't feel a need to specify what I meant until she looked at me inquiringly and asked, "Of what?"

"What I mean is who killed Harvey, and why?" I said as gently as I could.

She relaxed a little and continued to stare out the window, a thoughtful look in her dark eyes. "Isn't the who obvious, and the why for that matter?"

"Not to me, it isn't."

"Well, the police seem to think it was Nick Taylor." And they are the real authority her tone said. "Why is he running if he's not guilty?"

She had me there, so I changed course. "Did Harvey have any real enemies that you know of?"

Something unidentifiable stole across her drawn face as she again looked to the blue water. "It is characteristic of the human mind to hate the man who has injured."

Interpreting that to mean yes, I said, "Who would hate Harvey?"

She ignored the question, saying, "I'm going to have some more coffee. Would you care for a refill?"

"No thanks." I watched her shuffle into the kitchen, her left leg dragging behind as though it needed extra urging to accept her weight. The foot pointed in a slightly lateral direction. Her head and shoulders bobbed perceptibly with each step.

The water skiing accident had happened just before Ellen and Harvey's first wedding anniversary. Some say it was carelessness on Harvey's part. The propeller of the powerful engine had destroyed the muscles of Ellen's left thigh, leaving her permanently crippled. The young bride, who by all accounts had been quite athletic, even competing in Olympic trials, had gained forty pounds and disappeared from view for nearly two years.

Despite her infirmity, Ellen had a well-formed body and her skin-hugging leotard betrayed no slackness. She had certainly shed any weight that she'd gained. As I sat there I became aware of more things in the room. There was a rubber mat and a large inflated ball in the corner. Next to these were some foam blocks and a padded stool.

Returning with her coffee cup, Ellen noticed my gaze. "My yoga props," she said.

"What's the ball for?" I asked.

"You've never seen one of these?" She placed it in the middle of the room and effortlessly took a number of different positions on it, her limberness evident in the movements.

"What about that thing?" I said, pointing to the stool.

In one deft movement she did a headstand on it.

"You make that look easy." I noticed her well-developed upper arms and shoulders.

She gracefully came out of the headstand, and shrugged. "I do it every day." Back on the couch, she raised her bad leg off the floor. "Maybe I do it to make up for this."

Feeling a little embarrassed, I looked around the spacious room. "Do you plan to stay here, Ellen?"

"I don't know," she said, "I've got a lot of things to sort out before I make any decisions."

"It would be a shame to leave this beautiful home," I said.

Ellen had always been something of a recluse. One seldom saw her except maybe at the post office or at the odd wedding or funeral with Harvey. I remembered Rosie complaining that Ellen did all her shopping in the city, which miffed Rosie, who thought that supporting local business was second only to tithing to the church.

Ellen tucked her bad leg up underneath her and gazed out the window. "I haven't really decided anything yet. I may stay here, then again I may move back to Vancouver."

A boat burbled by. An older couple held fishing rods over the side.

"Did you know Andy Meyer very well?" I asked.

"No. No I didn't. He came out to speak to Harvey on occasion, but they met out in the office," she said, referring to the small cedar-clad structure set near the entrance to the property. "I think at one point Harvey was trying get him to buy a house, said he wanted to get him out of his ratty old trailer."

"Did Nick Taylor ever come here?"

"No," she said, as if stating the obvious. "As you probably know, he and Harvey didn't get along all that well."

I acknowledged that with a nod. "Do you have any idea why your husband disliked Nick so much?"

"No," she said a little tentatively, with just a hint of rebuke.

"I'm sorry, I didn't mean to make you uncomfortable."

"It's all right." She pulled the elastic out of her ponytail, allowing her hair to fall loosely around her attractive face. She took a deep breath as though she'd made up her mind about something. "Did you know Harvey's sister?"

I looked at her quizzically. "Harvey didn't have a sister."

"Do you remember Stella Bender?"

"Yeah, sure."

"That was Harvey's half-sister."

"What? But she was a Bender?"

"Stella's mother and Henry Kristoff had a short, not-so-sweet, affair."

I closed my mouth when I realized it was hanging open.

"It was a big family secret," Ellen said.

"They sure kept it well," I said, unlike Harvey's own philandering.

"Do you remember when Stella went away, apparently she was about sixteen?"

"Vaguely."

"She went to a home for unwed mothers in Regina."

"And you're saying...what are you saying?"

"That Nick was the father."

"What?" I frowned.

"Well, that's how Harvey told it."

I remembered the flamboyant Stella Bender. She was one of those girls who could only be described as, easy. She had a nice, if self-effacing personality, rich brunette hair, and a nicely put together figure, if a little on the plump side. One of those exuberant girls who feels she needs to keep everybody entertained, especially the boys. Nick may have been the father of her child, but I could think of a number of others that could just as easily qualify; and on one particular night, only because of my will of iron and Rosie's firm grip, was I not one of them.

"She never came back," I said, realizing I hadn't seen Stella since high school.

"Harvey said Stella wouldn't come back. He blamed Nick for it, blamed him for ruining her life."

"Where is she now?" I asked.

"Well, that's the kicker," Ellen said, "she's dead. Committed suicide."

"Damn." Another Fats Rodnicki. "And the child?" I asked.

"Harvey's been supporting him and the other kid, born a couple of years after the first."

So, he had a heart after all, old Harvey. "Who's going to support them now?"

"I don't know," she said with a shrug, suggesting she didn't much care.

Keeping a secret like that was not easy in a town rife with gossip. I wondered what Nick knew about all this.

"May I ask you a question?" she said.

"Of course."

"If Taylor gets off, do you think the real murderer will ever be caught?"

"I have no doubt about it," I said.

"What makes you so sure?"

"Maybe I'm naïve, but I believe that the guilty will get what's coming to them."

"The way of transgressors is hard," Ellen said dully.

"True enough," I agreed.

Ellen was silent, her eyes following the old couple in the boat as they drifted back and forth over the same spot. Then, as if coming out of a trance, she bunched up her hair and replaced the elastic. "I better get back to my yoga."

"And I should be getting home for dinner," I said.

Outdoors, the schnauzer welcomed me, sniffing at my shoes and forcing his snout into my hands looking for a treat. Ellen stood in the doorway as I drove out of the yard. I waved, but she just watched me drive away.

At Stuart's request, Rosie had made pizza for dinner. What Stuart calls Mother's mother of all pizzas, overflowing with salami, pepperoni and buried under three kinds of cheese. It screams heart attack, which is why Rosie makes another one, a little more health conscious, for us.

After wolfing down most of his pizza, Stuart hurried off to school showing no sign of having inhaled two pounds of protein, fat and carbohydrates. Over tea, I told Rosie about my visit with Gil Jarvis. She scoffed at my ignorance. "Those two have been squabbling for years."

"Yes, but did you know she moved out?"

A frown knitted Rosie's brow.

"He'd like to keep it quiet," I said. But the eager look on Rosie's face told me the cat was already out of the bag. "The cadet league will have to appoint somebody until Gil gets back on his feet."

"Poor Gil," Rosie said.

When I told her about Stella Bender, she said, "I knew there was something about that girl. Imagine that old man Kristoff."

"Harvey told Ellen that Nick was the father."

"Well, that explains a lot, eh." The look on Rosie's face seemed to cover it all. "Trouble seems to follow that damn Nick Taylor everywhere he goes."

Rosie's appraisal of Ellen Kristoff was predictable. "Anyone who spends so much time alone and isn't involved in the library or even the church must have psychological issues." Evidently Rosie had been doing some research in anticipation of Annie's counseling appointment.

"She's got a beautiful piano out there," I said. "Didn't she give piano lessons at one time?"

"Maybe to kids from the city," Rosie said, insinuating that Ellen was just too hoity-toity for small town Saskatchewan.

The following morning after picking up my mail, I was accosted by Eleanor Evanisky who literally stood me up against the cab of my truck with her verbal attack.

"You have no business snooping around out there. Don't you think that woman's been through enough?"

"What are you talking about?" I said.

"You know very well. Why don't you go back to chasing little girls?"

Just as I was about to respond, Dee Elliot, having seen the altercation from her office window called out, "Morning, Bart. Eleanor."

Eleanor, still carrying plenty of harangue, turned on her heel and flapped off.

"I wonder what got into her knickers?" Dee said, watching Eleanor hotfooting it down the street towards the R.M. Office. "By the look of things, I'm not sure you'd have got out of that one with your keester intact."

"You could be right," I said, "she was pretty worked up."

"About what?"

"I'm not sure. I think she was giving me the gears for going out to see Ellen Kristoff."

Dee looked at me inquiringly.

"I went out to Grayham Point yesterday."

"Yeah? Anything interesting?"

"Well, I found out why Harvey hated Nick."

"Come on in," Dee said with a reporter's zeal. "I've got some doughnuts and fresh coffee."

Seated across from Dee, coffee in hand, I told her about Stella Bender. Dee was fascinated and listened intently, prodding and probing to get the whole story. When I described the rest of my visit with Ellen—the yoga, the strange quotations—Dee asked, "Do you think she'll stick around?"

"If I were a betting man, I'd say she's gone by the end of the year."

Pulling out a manila folder, Dee said, "On another topic, I've got something to show you." She pulled out a fax. "Got this from the *Esterhazy Miner*."

I read the headline: *Assault Charges Laid after Game Ends in Brawl.* "Our boy, Gerald T.?"

"Yoop," Dee said, her mouth full of jelly doughnut.

"I guess his reputation is well founded."

"Here's another one." It read:

Gerald Meyer of Zeneta was arrested for causing a disturbance at the Spy Hill Hotel. Meyer's attack on two other patrons of the hotel's beverage room was described as brutal by an RCMP officer at the scene. The two injured men were taken by ambulance to hospital in Moosomin. Damage to the hotel's beverage room was estimated at one thousand dollars.

"According to the editor of *the Miner*," Dee said, "Gerald's been on a bender ever since his mother died a year ago. And it's not because he's all broken up over her passing either."

"What's it about?"

"Turns out Mom changed the will before she died. So after spending his whole life working on the farm, Gerald gets squat for his efforts."

"So who gets it?" I asked.

"Brother Andy," Dee said. "The lion's share, anyway." She smiled diabolically. "Cain and Abel?"

Would Gerald murder his own brother to get the inheritance? Could his inferred closeness to Andy be a fabrication? "Did you find out anything about how they got along?" I asked.

"Not really, but apparently Andy left the farm first chance he got, then after the old man died, Gerald handled the place by himself while Mom moved into town. I can certainly see why Gerald would have some expectations about the place."

"And to get stiffed after all that slugging," I said. "I'll tell you this, the guy I met wouldn't stand for it."

After indulging in one of Dee's Lucky Dollar doughnuts, I swung by the motel. No truck, of course, meant no Gerald. I went with my second guess, and sure enough, parked in front of the pub was the big black truck in all its dirty splendor. I surmised that since it was only eleven-thirty in the morning, Gerald would still be in reasonably good shape, but I surmised wrong. Even before the pub's boozy bouquet assailed my nostrils, I saw the mayhem that seemed to follow Gerald T. Meyer around. Tables and chairs were overturned and bottles and glasses littered the floor.

As my eyes became more accustomed to the dull light of the pub, I saw Gerald's meaty arm wrapped in a not so friendly embrace around Les Thatcher's balding head. Les's already florid complexion had turned beet red and he was gasping for air. A few regulars looked on from the opposite side of the bar. Even the ex-biker-bartender Steve Frazer kept his distance.

"What the hell's going on here, Les?" I said, as if he had any choice in the matter. I thought it would attract less ire than confronting Gerald directly.

Les looked at me as best he could, given his discomfiture, but it was obvious he was in no position to answer my query.

"Are you okay, Les?" I said. "Can you breathe?" Now even Gerald seemed to be waiting to hear Les's response. "Gerald, could you loosen up on him a bit, I'm not sure he can breathe." Gerald ignored me. "What's going on, anyway?"

"This fucking numb-nuts thinks he's a real smart ass," Gerald spat.

"Yeah?" I said. Les seemed to be breathing a little easier.

"He makes out like Andy was going to get fired." At the word fired, he sat Les down hard into a chair, releasing him from the headlock. "Says that's why he didn't get promoted to head greens keeper."

Les opened his mouth to protest, but Gerald squeezed his shoulder with such force that Les winced and only a stifled whimper came out.

"That's not what he was sayin', man." Steve Frazer said in Les's defense.

"You want some of this, man?" Gerald sneered back, holding up a fist.

"Gerald," I said, "it looks to me like there's no harm done. Why don't you let Les go on back to work." I looked at my watch as if to indicate Les's lunch hour was over. "Then maybe you and I can have a drink and chat. Whaddaya say?"

His eyes grew dull, and nearly closed. Clearly he'd already had more than a few. Suddenly he flung his arm in the direction of a corner table, and slurred to no one in particular, "Bring me a double."

I saw Les scurry out the door as we made our way to the table. Sitting down heavily, Gerald pulled out a crumpled pack of cigarettes and with some difficulty extracted one and lit it up. Steve brought over a double rye and coke and a bottle of Canadian for me. "This one's on the house," Gerald said, and Steve didn't bother to contradict him.

"You know, Gerald, as far as I know, Andy was doing fine out at the golf course. I never heard anything about him being let go, either." 'Course who knew what Harvey had planned. Just for good measure, I added, "He worked hard and did his job."

"Goddamn right. That fuckin' little pipsqueak," his head lolled toward the door, "better keep his mouth shut, or I'll shut the fucker for him." Gerald pounded the tabletop with his fist, knocking my beer bottle over on its side.

"I know Andy worked hard," I said, picking up the bottle and taking a short swig, "I'm sure you and your Dad put in a lot of hard time on that farm too."

"You Goddamned right we did." He gulped half his double rye into which he'd put a splash of coke, and said, "What the hell do you know?"

"I think you miss your brother."

Gerald's response was to kick a chair, sending it toppling over in the direction of the shuffleboard. Steve kept an eye on Gerald, but stayed behind the bar, where he and some of the regulars talked quietly.

"It must have been a real blow when you lost your dad," I said, hoping he wouldn't kick any more furniture.

"He was one hell of a farmer, eh, my dad," Gerald said, mournfully. "He always knew what kind of a year we would have. Good moisture, bad, strong markets or whatever." Smoke escaped Gerald's loose lips. "He did his research, eh. All winter he'd be studying the *Farmers Almanac* so he'd know what to plant and how much."

Light flooded the pub's entrance and Gerald's bleary eyes followed Corporal Fred Snell as he walked over to the bar. Steve Frazer gestured broadly at the overturned tables and chairs. A moment later Fred came over to where we sat.

"Mr. Meyer," he said, "can you tell me what's going on here?" Constable Reed now stood a few feet away, her right hand resting lightly on her Billy club. Fred's eyes landed on me for a second before returning to Gerald's sagging bulk. "I think you better come down to the station and sober up before you do any more damage. We'll talk about the rest later, okay?"

"What's the charge, *ociffer*?" Gerald's toothy grin was somehow desperate. He picked up his drink and drained it. Some of the remaining ice slipped through his sloppy lips and slid to the carpeted floor. "Let's go." He started struggling to his feet. When Fred took his arm in an attempt to help, Gerald wrenched out of his grasp and said drunkenly, "I can fuckin' get up myself." He then promptly tumbled sideways off his chair and joined his ice cubes on the soiled carpet.

Stepping out of the gloomy pub into the noonday sun, I found a note under the windshield of my pick-up. *No dinner today, gone to the city to see Annie. Back after supper. R.*

Since Stuart had baseball practice at noon, I was left to my own devices. As I was about to pull out of my parking spot a car stopped next to mine. From where I sat, I saw long legs reaching for the pedals, and a snug T-shirt that matched the blue sports car. Juliette Riskowsky.

She removed her sunglasses. Her eyes studied mine. There was a moistness behind them that could have come from the wind, but I thought differently. "How are you doing?" she asked.

"Good." I checked my rearview mirror for some reason. "So, you out for the weekend?"

"Yes, my seminar doesn't go on Fridays." She put the stick shift in neutral, let the clutch out and said, "We haven't really had a chance to talk about what happened."

"Right," I said.

She revved her motor a little, sending a puff of blue smoke down the street.

Even while berating myself, I said, "What are you doing for dinner?"

"I was planning to pick up a few things and have lunch at the cottage," she said. "Wanna join me?"

"Guess I could do that," I said. "Why don't I meet you there?"

"Okay, in say, half an hour? Anything in particular you like?"

"Don't go to any trouble on my account," I said.

She shifted deftly into first gear and roared away, and as she did so, I became aware of Eleanor Evanisky stationed directly across the street, in the shade of the pub, staring at me. She gave me a look that must have taken years to perfect. It said so many things, all of which spelled disaster for me.

Feeling like a kid caught with his hand in Mom's purse, I punched in my clutch and stepped on the gas. The truck lurched forward, the motor coughed, then stalled. Eleanor's glare didn't waver, only intensified. Tires squealing, I vaulted out of my parking spot on the next try, cutting off an on-coming car. I could almost hear Eleanor cackle as I straightened out and headed for the highway. I stopped and watched Stuart's ball team warming up at T.C. High for a few minutes. Stuart's coach had them doing some stretching and calisthenics before getting started. Stu played in the outfield, usually left, and had a good bat. He wasn't necessarily a big slugger, but nearly always got on base. Like in hockey, he was a real team player.

On my way to Pebble Beach, I passed Grayham Point. I could see that Kristoff's grass had yet to be cut. Ellen's car was not in the yard and there was no sign of Harvey's SUV. The schnauzer was on a rope, lying next to the house. Something compelled me to stop in. Maybe I just wanted to say hello to the dog. He gave his two or three yelps, before grinning and pulling on his rope in an attempt to get to me. As I patted his head, I noticed a big flashy boat tied to the dock. I walked down the sandy slope to the water's edge to get a closer look. It was a twenty-four foot, cherry-red Glastron, sporting twin hundred-horse Johnson's.

"Can I help you?" a gruff male voice called out. It was the old gentleman who I'd seen fishing the day before.

"I was looking for Ellen," I said, a little embarrassed, "do you know if she's around?"

"Well, her car's not here, so I doubt it." He watched me guardedly.

"I was just having a look at the boat here," I said, conversationally. "It's got all the bells and whistles, doesn't it?"

"We share the dock," he said. His fishing boat was tied up on the opposite side. There was a double boathouse next to it.

"Does Ellen use it?" I asked, nodding toward the big boat that had leather seating for eight.

"She does," he said.

"Does a little fishing, does she?"

Unsmiling, he said, "No, I don't think she does any fishing."

"Sorry," I said walking toward him, "my name's Bart Bartowski, and you are?"

He didn't make a move. "I know who you are. I'll tell Ellen you dropped by."

"Okay, thanks." I started toward my truck, then turned, "How's the fishing around here, anyway?"

"Why? You planning to go fishing?"

I shrugged. "Maybe."

"There are a couple of spots for jacks down here in the bay," he said, "but there isn't much good fishing on this end of the lake, except maybe over near Ireland's. There's a little hole over there, produces pretty good, spring and fall."

"I'll have to give it a try," I said.

"I guess this doesn't compare to what you're used to," he said.

"Well, every lake has its sweet spot. It's always nice to be able to wet a line right outside your door," I said. He didn't respond. "Well, I guess I better be running along."

"The name's Baumgartner, by the way," he said. "Frank Baumgartner. And Ellen, she never really used the boat much. Don't rightly know what she used it for when she did. Just cruising, I guess.

"Nice boat," I said.

He nodded, apparently unimpressed.

"Well, nice meeting you, Frank. You have a good day." He grunted. I gave the schnauzer a vigorous rubdown before I got into my truck.

Pebble Beach showed signs of coming to life. More cars, more people than there had been a couple of weeks earlier. I pulled in behind Juliette's MG.

"Welcome," she said as I stepped up on the deck. She had already set the table and was laying out cold cuts and fresh bread with pickles, mustard and other condiments.

Handing me a beer, she said, "It's nice to see you again." She held onto the long necked bottle. We had a playful tug o' war. "You must be thirsty," she said, finally letting go. The screen door slapped shut as she went inside, emerging a minute later carrying a tray laden with bowls of steaming soup.

While we ate our soup and sandwiches, Juliette told me about her seminar and about Professor Stevens who was teaching the course in philosophy. I found myself feeling just a little jealous as she described him as thirty-five, gorgeous and single, then relieved when she said, "I'm pretty sure he's gay."

"So, anything new on the murder?" She asked. "I haven't heard a word since I left."

"Well…and this is confidential, eh? But since you were there…it turns out that Andy didn't die from what we thought." I watched her suck mayonnaise off her thumb.

"What do you mean?" she asked.

"He was poisoned."

"Poisoned? But all that blood, that can't be right."

"That's what I said too, but apparently he'd been given the poison before he was slugged."

"Why would somebody do that?"

I told her Rosie's theory on the subject then slurped more beef broth.

Juliette ate a spoonful of soup, silently. "So I guess everybody in town knows that you and I...?"

"Yup," I said.

"Was it that woman we saw at the café?"

"Eleanor?" I thought about it for a moment. "Yeah, no doubt she spread the word, but it likely would have got out anyway. Funny thing you should mention Eleanor, I had a run-in with her earlier."

"What about?"

"I think she was miffed because I went out to talk to Ellen yesterday." I was still puzzled by her defense of Ellen Kristoff.

"Ellen?"

"Yeah, Harvey Kristoff's widow."

Juliette looked pained. "It must be horrible to have your husband murdered like that. How's she doing?"

"You'd have to ask someone who knows her a lot better than I do. She seems to be surviving though, looks good, anyway. She does this yoga and she's damn good at it. Even with that leg."

"What's wrong with her leg?" Juliette asked.

I told her about the water skiing accident.

"God, how awful," Juliette said.

"Yeah, and to make it worse, it happened less than a year after they were married."

"What a way to start a marriage."

"Yeah, no kidding, and she's been blessed with that limp ever since."

"Limp?" Juliette said.

"Handles it well, though," I said. "She's in good shape, considering." I remembered the snug leotard. "It's a real shame because I think it kind of isolates her." But I could tell Juliette wasn't listening.

"Bart," she said, biting her bottom lip.

"Yes," I said, mimicking her serious tone.

"I saw a woman with a limp."

I took a slug off my beer.

"You know when you told me to hop out of the van at White Pine. Well, I went into the café and sat down at the counter. I was sitting there for less than a minute or two when this woman came along and got into the car."

"What car?"

"Eleanor's car?"

"Really?" I said.

"Yeah, and she had a limp. That's why I remember her, because of the limp."

"What did she look like?"

Juliette looked pensive for a moment. "About forty, good figure, graying hair. But, mostly I remember the limp."

A shiver traveled the length of my spine. Could Ellen Kristoff have been at White Pine when Andy Meyer was murdered? Juliette sat wide-eyed, waiting.

"Can I use your phone?" When Stretch Strechuck came on the line, I said, "I need to ask you something, Stretch, something very important."

"Those heaters will be there, don't worry."

"It's not about the heaters," I said.

"Okay." He sounded relieved. "Fire away."

"Remember you told me you'd seen a woman with Andy Meyer at the pub in Wallburg?"

"Yeah, sure I remember."

"Can you describe her."

"What for?"

"Do you remember?" I persisted.

"Yeah, I s'pose. Let's see," he sucked air, "she was kind of medium, you know, medium everything."

I guess to Stretch that meant something, but to me it meant nothing at all.

"Details Stretch, height, age, any physical... characteristics, that sort of thing."

"Okay." He thought for a moment. "She was probably about thirty-five or forty. A redhead. The two of them were pretty close in height."

"Did you see her walk up to the bar, go to the washroom or anything like that?"

"Yeah, now you mention it, I did, and she didn't walk so good. Kinda gimped a little."

"Stretch," I paused in order to get his full attention, "you're sure the woman you just described is the one you saw playing VLTs with Andy Meyer?"

He paused for a moment, then said, "Yes, I'm damn sure it was."

Returning to the table out on the deck, I finished my sandwich and guzzled the rest of my beer. "I'm glad you're so observant, Juliette." I got up to leave.

She moved toward me and leaned in. "What's the rush?" I felt her arms go around my neck and the full length of her body press firmly up against me. God she smelled good. My natural instinct and the easiest thing on earth would have been to take her in my arms and... but then she pushed me away, and with a grin said, "Maybe when this is all over, you'll come by and pay me another visit."

Once again, I was relieved, but dissatisfied at the same time.

18

On the drive into town I decided it was time to turn the tables on Ms. Eleanor Evanisky. I found her on her knees in the front yard. She was planting a variety of brightly coloured annuals in the two small beds that hemmed in her small bungalow. Eleanor was not what you'd call flamboyant in her approach to landscaping. She kept everything under strict control with deeply cut borders around each bed reinforced by four-inch vinyl edging to ensure nothing went astray. The lone tree, a nice white birch, was similarly contained at the centre of the front yard. The lawn would have made a greens keeper proud, cut uniformly to an exacting length with neither dandelion nor clover visible in the lush turf.

Eleanor swung her head and torso around at the sound of my truck door slamming. She struggled to her feet, aiming her broadside at me as she did so. By the time she was fully erect, I was standing next to her.

"Bart Bartowski." She said my name as though it were a profanity.

"Eleanor," I greeted her.

"Well? What do you want?"

"When Andy Meyer was murdered," I said, "you were at White Pine Beach."

She stood mute and appeared to have stopped breathing. Her left eye twitched.

"Were you alone?"

"Why should I answer that? You have no business coming to my home and interrogating me. Do you hear?" She squeezed out the last words breathlessly.

"What do you have to hide, Eleanor?"

"Get out of my yard," she said sternly, as though gaining strength by the power of private property. "If you don't go right now," she bellowed, walking towards the house, "I'm calling the police."

"Okay, call the police. I'm sure they'd love to hear how you were out at White Pine with Ellen Kristoff at the precise time that Andy Meyer was murdered." Her progress toward the house slowed with each word.

She turned and said, "What do you want?"

It was my turn to stay mute.

"Damn you." Looking around to see if any neighbors were about, she said, "Come inside." I followed her to the side door of the bungalow.

"Tell me this," she said, holding me at bay in the porch, "why are you tormenting her? Hasn't she suffered enough?"

"Has she?"

"You self-righteous bastard," Eleanor hissed. "I wondered to what depths you would sink to prove that Nick Taylor innocent."

"Eleanor, do you have any idea what you've gotten yourself in to?"

"What are you talking about?"

"What do you think Ellen was doing at White Pine that day?"

Eleanor sank into a chair at the kitchen table. Her complexion, which had been a rosy pink outdoors, had suddenly become so pallid that I felt compelled to fill a glass with tap water and set it on the table in front of her. Eyeing it, she pushed it aside and turned to a cabinet behind her from which she extracted a half-full bottle of rye. She filled a shot glass and drained it in one swallow, then filled it again.

"I drove Ellen to White Pine, yes it's true," she said. "I thought we were going for coffee and a friendly visit." Eleanor fortified herself with another sip of the whiskey. "We'd say hello on the street and she sometimes brought papers to the office for Harvey, but she'd never called before. So I was pleased for the company, and besides, she'd just lost her husband and all, and Lord knows, after losing my job..." Eleanor breathed deeply, drew herself up and continued. "We sat on the balcony looking out on the lake, enjoying our coffee; it was a lovely day." The pleasant memory showed fleetingly on her plump face. "I went for refills and when I returned, she was gone. I assumed she was in the washroom, but," Eleanor sniffed, "after waiting for twenty minutes, I went to check and there was no one there. So, I paid for the coffees and went out to wait for her in my car."

"You had no idea what was going on?"

"What *was* going on?" Eleanor cried. "Where *was* she?"

I waited for a moment before answering. "I think you know."

Eleanor's shoulders slumped.

"How long was it before you saw her again?" I asked.

"I waited another ten or fifteen minutes. She came around the side of the café and acted as though everything was normal. As though she hadn't disappeared for over half an hour without a word." Eleanor emptied the shot glass between her quivering lips. "She was smiling. I could smell her perfume. She must have applied some just after..." Eleanor's face reflected the appalling thought.

"You drove her home?"

Eleanor nodded dolefully.

"Have you spoken to her since that day?"

"No," Eleanor said, alarmed. "I don't dare."

"How did you know I'd been to see her?" I asked.

"I was just driving by," she said not very convincingly.

I looked around. The house was spotless; everything in a state of readiness, but despite cheerful curtains and fresh flowers on the table, a gloom seemed to hang about the place. I could see a large picture of Eleanor's son on the mantelpiece in the living room. After her husband died, years earlier, Eleanor had devoted herself to her son. But when he graduated from engineering school, he moved to the States and later to jobs all over the world. Eleanor was a lonely woman and other people's business was a natural, if disaffecting diversion. But it would have to suffice until her son returned.

"Eleanor, this will have to come out."

She looked stricken.

"It's the only way," I said.

"Oh, my," she said, then swallowed the rest of her rye.

"And believe me, it'll make you feel a lot better."

Her glassy eyes strayed to the picture of her son, and before I left, there might have been a hint of hope in them, maybe even a little of the old tittle-tattle.

I stopped at home to leave a note for Rosie and make a call to Frank Baumgartner who answered on the tenth ring.

"I was working on my outboard," he said. "Damn thing just won't idle right."

"Mr. Baumgartner, I'd like to come out and have a word with you, if you have a few minutes."

"You must know something about these damn things?"

"Yeah, a little," I said.

"Well, come on out then."

Ten minutes later, I arrived at the Baumgartner's house at Grayham Point. I found Frank in his boat hunched over a fifteen horsepower Suzuki. The engine cap was off and lay nearby cradling his tools. "Howdy," I said, as I reached the dock.

He grunted without taking his eyes off his work. The odor of gasoline was potent.

"So, she won't idle, eh?" I said.

"Nah. As soon as I get down to trolling speed, she quits. I've cleaned the carburetor, replaced the fuel filter and adjusted this damn idle 'till I'm sick of it."

"Mind if I have a look?"

He rose stiffly and stepped out of the twelve-foot aluminum boat. "Help yourself."

I picked up the screwdriver. "I wanted to ask you something," I said. "I hope you won't think it's out of line."

"Get this thing running right, I'll tell you anything," he said. "I want to get out there and do some fishing."

As I pulled the spring out of the idle adjuster, I said, "Mr. Baumgartner, did you ever see Andy Meyer out visiting the Kristoffs?"

"Well," he said, removing his Crooked Lake Fishing Derby cap, "I wouldn't have known who Andy Meyer was until his picture appeared in the paper. Of course that was after he was dead. In any case, it struck me that I had seen him, and not so long ago either."

I kept working on the idle adjuster.

"I saw him and Ellen taking off in the Kristoff's boat. Saw him again when he drove Ellen's car into the garage later the same day."

"Was that before or after Harvey's murder?"

"It was after, a few days after." I remember wondering who the fella was with Ellen.

I just kept my mouth shut, and holding the valve open on the gas hose, I pumped a little gas out of the tank.

"I was out here working on my dock. I saw them through the open door of the garage."

I squeezed some more fuel out of the gas tank. "What were they doing?"

"Unloading. Suitcases, other stuff too. I figured he was helping her out. I remember there was a giant beach ball."

"You know what," I said, "it looks to me like you have a blockage in your gas line." He peered at it from the dock. "Not enough gas getting through at idling speeds."

Frank's look went from disbelief to anger as he said to himself, "You goddamned old fool. Here I am spending half the morning buggering around with the motor, when it's my head that needs examining."

"Don't be too hard on yourself," I said, "it happens to all of us."

"Just goes to show you," he said in frustration, "age and wisdom don't necessarily go hand in hand."

We connected his spare hose, started the motor and re-adjusted the idle.

"Well I'll be damned," he said, "purrs like a kitten." He shook his head. "Sure glad you came along. I'd have been here all day muckin' around." He put his fishing rod and tackle box into the boat.

"Good luck," I said, and as Frank pulled away from the dock, a yoga ball rolled through my mind.

In preparation for the Nick Taylor benefit, the Rec Centre had been transformed into a mini gambling casino. Christmas lights had been wrapped around every tabletop, doorframe, pillar and post. Some even hung imaginatively in space interspersed with shiny disco balls. It was at the Taylor fundraiser that I again saw Gerald T. Meyer. I hardly recognized him under the black lights at Bowling for Dollars where he was throwing mostly luminescent gutter balls. Before I could get over to talk to him, I'd been dragged to my post at the Wheel of Fortune. In fact every last member of the old-timers' hockey team had volunteered to help out in aid of their long-time teammate. While Carlton's Casino took care of the real gambling, we old-timers, in our splendid green hockey sweaters, looked after bingo, Wheel of Fortune and Bowling for Dollars.

When I finally got a chance to talk to Gerald, I was surprised to see he was clean-shaven, his hair was neatly combed and he appeared to be wearing a whole new set of duds. But what surprised me most was that he was clear-eyed and sober.

"Care for a drink?" he said, pointing to the bar where players' wives were serving beverages to the thirsty gamblers. I chose a coffee in a styrofoam cup while Gerald grabbed a juice box.

I recalled the last time we'd shared a drink. "So, you winning?" I asked.

"Nah," he said. "Can't bowl worth a shit and I've lost way too much money playing poker to go near those black jack tables."

"I'm a little surprised to see you here. I'd have thought a fundraiser for Nick Taylor would be the last place you'd show up."

"Nothing much else to do in this burg."

Not like the thriving metropolis of Zeneta, I thought. "It's a little noisy in here," I said, "I wonder if we could step outside for a few minutes?"

He looked at me circumspectly for a moment. "Sure, why not?" He crushed his empty juice box and tossed it into a wastebasket. "I'm pretty much done here, anyway."

The light was waning in the evening sky. We slowly ambled down the sidewalk towards Dr. Okianec Park at the centre of town.

"Did you know your brother was involved with Harvey Kristoff's wife?" I said cutting right to the chase.

Gerald stopped and looked at me. "Whaddaya mean involved?"

I left no doubt as to my meaning.

Turning sullen Gerald said, "So what?"

"Well, that would put him right in the middle of things, eh?"

"What the hell are you talking about?"

"You know, love triangle, that sort of thing. Maybe Harvey found out."

Gerald thought about that for just a moment. "That's bullshit." He turned and faced me. "I know what you're doing. You're tryin' to get your friend off at my brother's expense, but I'll tell you something mister, there's no way in hell that's gonna happen."

"I understand that before your mother died, she changed your father's will and left most of the farm to Andy."

Gerald staggered a little. "How the fuck did you know that?"

I ploughed on. "It must have made you pretty upset. After all, you told me you were the one who stayed and worked that farm."

"You goddamn right I did. Look, Bartowski…"

"And Andy, he just buggered off?"

Gerald shook his head mournfully. "He couldn't have cared less about the place."

"You stayed, though."

"You damn right I did. And after Dad was gone, I stayed some more. If it weren't for me…"

"Yet Andy is the one who ends up with the lion's share."

He looked forlornly at the cairn at the centre of the park. It had a plaque on it, commemorating Derf Okianec's fifty years in Crooked Lake. "She didn't even leave me enough to survive on," he said.

"That's not what your dad had intended."

"No." He took a shallow breath. "It was her. She was always against me. No matter what I did, I just wasn't good enough. Only Andrew lived up to her expectations. Only Andrew went to Tech in Saskatoon, and traveled all over creation. And how did he pay for it?" Gerald slapped his chest. "From my stinkin' hard work, and Dad's, that's how. I froze my ass off every winter in that machine shed overhauling equipment. We never once had a breakdown, at seeding time or harvest.

When the prices went into the toilet, did I give up? No way. I stuck it out." He pointed a finger at me to emphasize the point. The fingernail was clean, I noticed. "Dad, he appreciated it. He knew what it took to run a farm in this day and age. He knew that every time you turn around there's some son-of-a-bitch trying to take you over, whether it's a bank or your goddamned neighbour. And then what does my very own mother go and do?" There was a bitter ring to his words. "All I wanted was half, just half so I could go on running the farm the way I always did. But Andy, he wouldn't listen to me. 'Let's sell it,' he said." Gerald groaned. His eyes turned cloudy.

"I just couldn't, wouldn't let that happen. I came up to Crooked Lake to see him and try to make him understand. I went to his trailer." Gerald's vacant look suggested he was no longer seeing me. "But he wouldn't listen. He didn't seem to care; it was like he was drunk or something. He didn't seem to care about anything." Gerald clenched his fists. "I got mad. I shook him, but he kept saying he had other plans, he was going to be a big shot. Said soon he wouldn't need my scrubby little farm. Said he'd be living in the lap of luxury. He said he never wanted to see the farm again. Why not sell it? He told me to get out, he didn't want to hear anymore of my dad's worn out drivel." Gerald's head listed sorrowfully. "My dad's worn out drivel."

"I lost my temper. I pushed him, I pushed him hard." Gerald banged his fists on his legs mechanically. "His head hit the toilet, it was such an awful crack, then he didn't move. I didn't mean to hurt him. God knows, I didn't mean to kill him," Gerald bellowed. The big man's eyes squeezed shut, the veins swelled purple in his forehead, and from that deep place where he stored his huge belly laugh, came gushes of sorrow and regret. His legs gave out and he collapsed onto the park bench. He covered his face with his enormous hands and through them blubbered, "I'm sorry, Andy. I'm so sorry."

19

I should have told Gerald about the poison and that he hadn't been responsible for his brother's death, but for some reason, I didn't. Instead, I left him to his misery and drove out to Grayham Point.

"Please don't bother, really," I said as Ellen began spooning chili into a saucepan. She picked up a knife with a long serrated blade and cut thick slices of white bread.

"Since Harvey's gone," she said, "I haven't done much cooking, especially for a hungry man." She gave me an appraising glance.

I noticed the casserole dishes still lay on the counter top. We left the chili heating on the stove and went into the living room.

"Care for a drink?" she said.

"No thanks, I'm driving," I said.

She went behind the bar where she mixed a gin and tonic for herself. She knocked back half her cocktail in one swallow.

"That's a nice boat you've got out there," I said, nodding toward the dock.

"That was Harvey's boat."

"You don't use it?" I asked.

She made a curt movement of her head that didn't mean yes, but didn't mean no, either.

I said, "Great living right on the lake."

She took another drink. "It's all right. Harvey liked it. He'd bring clients over and show them around in his big boat. He thought it impressed them," she said, getting up off the couch. "I'll be right back." A few minutes later she returned and set a tray down on the dining room table. A stained glass lantern that hung above it cast an amber glow; the lantern's design resembled a crucifix, even down to the stylized nails.

Ellen invited me to take my place in front of a large bowl of steaming chili that she set on a place mat depicting mountains and ocean. Slices of buttered bread were piled on a small plate next to it. Ellen sat at the end of the long table, her drink in front of her.

"Smells delicious," I said, sniffing audibly.

"It's vegetarian. I hope you don't mind."

"Could've fooled me." I took another whiff.

"Lentils have a meaty aroma," she said.

"I've never had lentils," I said. "Healthy, I bet." Steam billowed upward as I stirred the hot chili. "Did Harvey like lentils?"

"Harvey," she hooted. "Not Harvey, I had to put meat in front of him three times a day or he'd be a bear."

"A little hard to please, was he?"

Her skin looked unhealthy in the lantern light and deepened the lines on her face. "You might say that. He had only one way of seeing things, his way. His drinks," she lifted her own, "had to have two ice cubes in them, no more, no less. His steak had to be oozing just the right amount of blood. And if I let poor Kitsilano in the house," she patted the schnauzer that lay at her feet, "I'd never hear the end of it."

"I can't help but think in a way you're not entirely unhappy he's gone."

"I never said that," she replied sharply. The colour rose in her cheeks, she looked off towards the lake and inhaled deeply. "Despite all that, Harvey was a good provider." She waved an arm, indicating the good life all around her. "He allowed me to pursue my interests and didn't judge me too harshly for my own little proclivities or for that matter," she waved her damaged leg, "infirmities. Harvey had some shortcomings, but we all do, right? I bet even you're not perfect."

"You're right there," I laughed, "just ask Rosie."

Behind the bar once again, she poured herself another gin and tonic, ignoring an ice-cube that escaped the ice tongs and shattered on the marble tile that surrounded the bar. "So, it looks like your amateur detecting hasn't helped Nick Taylor much."

"That has yet to be seen, don't you think? Means, motive and opportunity all have to be proven. Any shadow of a doubt and…" I let the words float.

"From what I understand," she stirred her drink with a ringed index finger, "he had the murder weapon in his golf bag, that's means; he blamed Harvey for losing his job, and screwing his wife, that's motive; and he has no alibi, that's opportunity."

"Why would Nick kill your husband, though? Find the person who would really gain from Harvey's death and you probably get closer to the mark." I brought the cloth napkin to my lips.

Her glance touched fleetingly on my bowl. She adjusted the ginger scarf she wore around her neck and tugged on the cuffs of her white cotton blouse primly. "And do you have some idea who that might be?"

"Well, now that you ask." I felt a fierce anxiety invade my gut.

Ellen's inquiring gaze never left my face. Finally she said, "I wondered why you were here. You think it was me, don't you?"

"There's always room for error," I said.

"You bet your ass there is," she said.

"None-the-less," I said, "if I might hypothesize?"

After a moment's hesitation, she nodded her head nonchalantly, as though her life didn't depend on it.

Quoting Frank Hendrickson, I said, "There are mainly three motives for murder: money, passion and power. Find the person who possess one or more of these motives, and you've got your man, so to speak."

I rubbed my hands together while organizing my thoughts, then stopped when I realized it might look too much like glee. "Harvey was brash, a bully, maybe even abusive," Ellen's expression remained unchanged, "and he played around. But like you said, one thing Harvey did do well was make money. Let's assume that rumour has it correct, and you did sign a prenuptial agreement before you got married to Harvey. Now, if you left him, likely all you'd take with you would be the clothes on your back and your yoga ball."

"You seem to know Harvey so well," she said in mock astonishment.

"But if Harvey were to conveniently shuffle off to Buffalo, you would have it all. Including the two quarters of land he was about to give away to Stella Bender's offspring."

She was unable to hide the surprise on her face.

"Yes, I know about that too."

"You know it all, don't you?" she said.

I made a gesture of modesty and then continued. "Andy Meyer is lonely and is royally pissed that Ron

Diccum gets the job that should have been his. You lure Andy in with just the right bait. Soon he's hooked and you play him like the sucker he is."

A sheen of moisture had developed on Ellen's upper lip. "You have quite a fertile imagination."

I pressed on. "You know that the Rileys have all but abandoned their cottage and are going to list it with Harvey when they return from visiting their daughter in Germany. That leaves Riley's Rest for you and Andy to play house in, giving you plenty of time to convince him that his dreams have come true. Poor Andy must have thought he'd died and gone to heaven. But what he didn't realize was he was being used the whole time. You impersonated Wilma Taylor, a red wig, a nice green suit. Unfortunately, Wilma didn't cooperate and instead of being on her way home from work with no alibi, she was visiting her sick mom at the hospital in P.A."

Ellen's round eyes narrowed perceptibly.

"And the disguises didn't stop there, did they? You got Andy all dolled up, and witnesses saw *you* working in the garden at the time of Harvey's death."

"But, when your plan to implicate Wilma doesn't pan out, you decide to shift the blame to Nick. You've already got his seven iron that Andy lifted from his bag in the pro-shop. Once the deed is done, and having finished with Riley's Rest, you are about to clear out when I stumble in."

I imagined the scene for a moment and wondered, "Did you have to haul my ass out to the truck all by yourself, or was Andy there to help?" I swallowed dryly. She made no response. "After leaving me for dead at the bottom of Ireland's Ravine, you and Andy clear Rileys out for good. How's that so far?" I said.

"You have a lot of nerve," she said, "I've gotta give you that." She picked up her empty glass and rattled her ice-cubes. "I think I'm going to need another one of these."

Again I found myself rubbing my hands together. When Ellen returned to her seat at the dining room table, I said, "Under the guise of a friendly gesture, you invite Eleanor Evanisky, another friendless soul, out for coffee and that's when your relationship with Andy comes to a poisonous end. But not before you use him one last time to make a phone call and put Nick Taylor at the scene. You plant the wig and scarf and your job's done.

With Harvey out of the way, you get the money, you get rid of a man you detest passionately, and you have the power to direct your own destiny—money, passion and power."

Her lips formed a smile, but her eyes were smoldering. "You think you can prove any of this?" she said. But before I could answer, she staggered down the hall towards the bathroom. "You can tell me all about it when I get back. Help yourself to a drink."

I pushed the bowl of chili away from me and resisted the temptation to take a bite out of the chewy white bread. I left the table and looked around the adjoining living room. During my earlier visit, it seemed there was something missing. Now I realized what it was. There were no pictures, no family memorabilia, not even a picture of Ellen or Harvey. Actually there was one picture, sitting on the big screen TV, an elaborately framed blow-up of Kitsilano. I had a feeling the schnauzer hadn't sat there while Harvey was around.

Out on the bay, a glowing sunset had set the water aflame. The sheer brilliance of it captured my attention, that is, until I saw Ellen's white blouse in the deep shadow of the boathouse. I wondered what the hell she was doing out there until I heard the twin engines growl to life. I rushed to the door, but only in time to watch her roar away from the dock and head toward the darkening eastern shores of Crooked Lake.

20

"Fred," I said into the phone, "it was Ellen Kristoff."

"What?"

"Ellen Kristoff killed her husband, then got rid of her accomplice."

"Wait a minute. Are you saying that…what are you saying?"

"Ellen murdered Harvey, with Andy's help. Then, she poisoned Andy to shut him up. Now she took off."

"What do you mean, took off?"

"I'm at her house. After I confronted her with the evidence, she took off in her boat. She's out on the lake."

"What evidence do you have?" Fred asked, doubtfully.

"Trust me, Fred. She's the one."

"You better not be full of shit. Just stay where you are and don't do anything stupid," he warned.

Ten minutes later Fred and Constable Reed walked in the door of the Kristoff house. Fred was talking into his cell phone. "She left here about twenty minutes ago." He looked at me and said, "What kind of boat?"

"Twenty-four foot fiberglass with twin hundred's," I said.

He repeated the description into the cell phone. "Get out as soon as you can. Let me know if you spot her." Fred hung up. Then he examined the room closely. I watched as he took in the piano, the yoga equipment and the picture of Kitsilano. He picked up a glass off the dining room table. Sniffing it, he said, "She was drinking?"

"Yeah. She had at least a couple or three gin and tonics while I was here. Probably more before I arrived."

"And you?"

"Just a bowl of chili," I said innocently, pointing to my untouched bowl on the table.

Fred's cell rang. "Snell here." He listened. "We may have something. Constable Reed and I are at the home of Ellen Kristoff and she appears to be taking evasive actions after being confronted with some," Fred looked over at me, "evidence, suggesting she murdered her husband and possibly Andy Meyer too."

He listened for a few moments then hung up. "Hutt's on his way," he said to Reed. Then he turned to me. "Now before he gets here, I want to know what you've got."

I described my conversation with Ellen and gave Fred a thumbnail sketch of the evidence I had gathered. By the end of it, Fred was convinced that Ellen could be deemed a suspect.

When Sergeant Hutt arrived, he said, "What's the situation?"

Fred answered, "I've deployed men to Pebble Beach and the Potato River, and I've ordered the patrol boat back out on the lake."

Hutt and Klassen scowled and grimaced in turn as Snell passed on my thumbnail sketch. The detectives grudgingly reserved judgment, at least for the moment

Again Snell's phone rang. "Jesus Christ," he said. "Okay, we'll get to you as soon as we can." His look was one of disbelief as he ended the call. "Looks like Bart was right. The patrol spotted her off White Pine. When they put the light on her she slowed down, but at the last second gunned it, and rammed them. Renwick was thrown out of the boat."

"Is he okay?" Hutt asked.

"Yeah, but now the goddamned thing won't start. They're out of commission." Dialing, he said, "We shoulda got that thing fixed properly. I'm calling in P.A. Who knows where this thing is going?"

I slipped out the back door and headed over to Frank Baumgartner's. TV light flickered off his living room wall. He opened the door cautiously at my insistent knock.

"Yes?" A pair of spectacles rested on the bridge of his nose. When he recognized me, he said, "Little late, isn't it?"

"Sorry to disturb you, Fred. There's a problem next door and I need to borrow your boat."

"What kind of problem?"

"Ellen Kristoff is in trouble."

"What kind of trouble?"

"The worst kind."

He looked at me blankly.

"What is it, dear?" Frank's wife, dressed in her nightgown, stood at the entrance to the living room.

"Not sure yet, honey," he said gently. He stepped outside and closing the door, said, "Now, what the hell's this all about?"

I explained as we walked down to the dock.

When I began untying his twelve-foot fishing boat, he said, "Not that one."

With the lights on and the boathouse door droning open, Frank's other boat came into view. The classic teak speedboat was definitely not built for fishing, it had room for four passengers and not much else. The boat descended the cleverly built rail system that allowed Fred to single-handedly launch her in less than a minute.

With the big inboard engine now idling, I said, "Okay Frank, I'll take it from here."

"She doesn't go anywhere without me," he said. His tone suggested there was no point in arguing, so I climbed aboard and we shoved off. Frank picked up a handset and spoke into it. "Hi honey."

The two-way radio squawked.

"Everything's fine," he said into his mouthpiece. "Bart here just needs a lift. I'll be back shortly. You go on back to bed now." With that, he pulled a camouflage hat over his thinning, gray hair and said, "Where to?"

I decided to play a hunch. "Let's head for Pebble Beach."

The speedboat skimmed along the glassy water effortlessly and before long we were nearing White Pine. We came within a few hundred feet of the disabled police boat. They flashed their floodlight, but with a look from me, Frank swept on by. In another ten minutes we were approaching Pebble Beach.

"Pull 'er back a bit," I said to Frank. He moved the throttle back a third. The boat surfed on its wake, then he pulled it back another third. Lights glimmered on the water, reflecting beachfront cottages. Frank guided the boat toward Riley's dock. As we got within fifty yards of it, we could see Ellen's abandoned Glastron drifting a few feet from the wharf, riding low in the water. Apparently the collision had done some damage.

I whispered, "Turn it off, Frank." He did so, then reached for a paddle. I did the same and we paddled soundlessly toward the dock. I hopped out, taking the end of the bow rope with me and tied her off. "Stay here," I said. Frank nodded as he reached to secure the stern line.

I hurried off the dock and moved as quietly as I could towards the dark cottage. Before I reached it, I heard scuffling behind me. Turning, I saw Ellen stand in her boat and point what looked like a rifle at Frank's chest.

"I need your boat, Frank," she said. "Get out and hurry it up."

He didn't move. I was hoping to God he wouldn't do anything foolish in an effort to save his boat.

"Move," she shrieked.

Frank stepped gingerly onto the dock, while Ellen climbed into his boat.

"Okay, Bartowski, get over here." She kept the gun pointed at Frank.

"Ellen," I said as calmly as I could, "you don't want to do this. There's got to be a better…"

A flash exploded from the gun barrel, sending shock waves through the night.

"Please don't," I heard Frank whimper.

"Get in the boat, Bart," Ellen said. "Now."

I walked the planks of the old dock on wobbly knees.

"In the back," she said, waving the gun at me. A moment later, hands tied behind my back, I was securely lashed to the boat's mooring ring, and unable to move from the rear seat.

"Ellen," I said, "I know you had your reasons. He was abusive. You had no way out. I'm sure all that would be taken into…"

"Shut up," she growled, and gave me a vicious blow to the forehead with the butt end of the heavy rifle. I saw stars, and they weren't in the heavens. The pain helped me fully comprehend that my fate now rested in the hands of a desperate murderer. If confronting her with my hypothesis hadn't been the smart thing to do, then chasing after her was downright dumb.

I could just make out Frank standing on the shore. The light had now all but disappeared. A pungent, watery smell assailed my nostrils, a reminder that the lake was a living and a dying thing. The motor came to life and Ellen, holding the rifle, a scoped thirty-thirty, untied the bowline and shifted into reverse. As she did so, the glassy crash of pebbles came from down the beach.

A spotlight cut a hole in the darkness and played first on Frank, then panned along the dock to where Ellen knelt on the driver's seat. An amplified voice said, "This is the police. Bring the boat back to the dock and turn your engine off." Ellen ignored them. "Stop, or you will be fired upon."

"I've got company," Ellen shouted, shifting into neutral.

The spotlight moved to where I sat immobilized in the rear seat. I heard the policemen's muttered curses.

"Return to the dock, now," the amplified voice warned.

All at once, a blast from Ellen's rifle shattered the spotlight. This precipitated a yelp and more profanities from the beach.

Flashes blazed out of the darkness. I heard bullets whistle by above our heads. Ellen slammed the throttle down; the boat reeled away from the shore as more flashes lit up the night. As we continued to accelerate, I asked myself: why didn't I listen to Rosie?

Ellen raced across the lake, then turned east, staying just off the north shore. She looked back at me and howled over the roaring engine, "How does it feel to be the big detective now?" Again Rosie's words echoed in my ears. Ellen's tired face had turned savage. Her wild eyes glinted and her steely hair whipped about her shoulders. "You can't play with fire and not get burned," she said. "But you didn't learn that, not even at the bottom of that ravine."

As she spoke, I tugged on my constraints, which only made them tighter. My forehead pounded and warm blood dripped off the end of my nose. It was then I recalled Ellen's Olympic sport, biathlon: skiing and marksmanship. She was undeniably a good shot.

"You know, had you left well enough alone, things would have worked out just fine," she said. "We'd have been rid of a couple of assholes, and we all could have carried on living our boring small town lives. But you had to interfere."

Ellen steered a hard left, slowed, and kept very near the treed bank on the north shore. The twilight illuminated the centre of the lake, leaving its edges in darkness.

"What do you hope to accomplish?" I said. "Quit, before it's too late."

"Shut up," she screamed. "Don't you tell me what to do; not like him."

"Please, Ellen."

"You have no idea what I went through with that devil. Do you know what he said after he destroyed my life with his goddamned motorboat? He said, 'now what are you good for?' Imagine?" The words clearly stung her, even now. "I put up with that monster for seven years, and here he is giving all that money to those Stella Bender bastards. Nick Taylor wasn't the father, you know. It was fucking Harvey, Harvey was the father. That's why he's so goddamned concerned. They're his bastards, both of them. Then the prick tells me he's going to dump me?" she said, with a mirthless laugh.

"Ellen, there are police all around the lake and more coming." I gave her my meaningful look, hoping it might cut through the darkness. "The smart thing would be to give yourself up."

"There's one thing you're forgetting, Mr. Detective." Her sardonic grin was revealed by the dashboard light. "I've got a hostage."

It hadn't occurred to me until that moment that I was a hostage. What did it mean? It meant she needed me alive, I thought with relief. But for how long?

Her glare was cold and her voice icy as she said, "And if I go down, you go down too."

Well, that cleared things up. She was crazy. She was a reclusive, psychopathic lunatic who took the lives of two men as if they were nothing more than annoyances. I could see no way out for her and I tried to ignore the implication for me.

Again I struggled with the rope, but it held fast. I couldn't stand, I couldn't turn. I was trapped in the seat. Then, over the idling engine, I heard the chopping sound of a helicopter. It must have flown in from P.A. A powerful beam of light illuminated huge swaths of water as the chopper flew a zigzag pattern over the lake. In less than a minute it would spot us.

Ellen realized it too. She veered sharply left and pushed the throttle to full, running the boat mercilessly into the muddy bank. Before I knew what was happening, she wrenched on the rope, pulling me to my feet. Pointing the rifle at me, she said, "Okay. It's time to play hostage." And with that, she crosschecked me over the side and into the water.

I found my head submerged, the breath knocked out of me, my hands tied behind me, and my feet in a muddy abyss. Just as I experienced the dreadful sensation of breathing in water, I felt a sharp tug on the rope. It was just enough to raise my head above the surface. I gulped for air. Coughing and spitting, I attempted to get to my feet but fell forward. Ellen held onto the rope, alternately pulling then pushing me until I collapsed, face first, onto muddy earth. As I turned over I saw the spotlight from the helicopter zig when it should have zagged, missing us completely.

Ellen also watched, a glow of satisfaction on her face. She pulled on the rope that held my hands behind me and I struggled to stand, then stumbled backward through the underbrush. My head collided brutally with a tree and before long I was again bound to an immovable object. Silhouetted against the glistening water, Ellen returned to the boat. She shoved off and climbing aboard, started the motor.

Was that it? Was my ordeal over? Thank God, thank you Lord. I will stay home. I'll fix those stairs until they're the best damn stairs in town. As I continued swearing oaths, what I thought was an apparition climbed out of the water, but it was no apparition. With the rifle resting casually on her shoulder, Ellen watched Frank's classic Chris Craft speed, unoccupied, across the lake.

Then I heard the strangest thing, the chorus of the old hymn, *Rock of Ages*. The music was interrupted when Ellen said, "Yes?" into her cell phone. After a few more affirmatives, she shouted, "You goddamn well better be there, do you hear me?"

I heard the bolt action of the rifle as Ellen pushed a cartridge into the breach. "All right Bart, like the song says, it's time to say goodbye." She turned and pointed the thirty-thirty at my forehead.

I closed my eyes. Why didn't I listen to Rosie? I didn't have to be here. I didn't need to get involved. I could have just stayed home and worked in the garden, done some things with the kids. A cold gush of guilt washed over me, and then…click.

I opened my eyes and watched as Ellen examined the rifle. She ejected a couple of rounds, breached another cartridge, then aimed at my forehead again. Click. Click.

"Well, fuck this," she said," and viciously rammed the butt of the rifle into my left knee. While I'm sure I cried out, I didn't hear it. I was too busy absorbing the fact that I was still alive. I was actually enjoying the exquisite pain that streaked up and down my leg. Then she clobbered me over the head and I was spared any further enjoyment.

I don't know how long I was out, but when I came to, she was gone and I was still tied to the tree. As my head cleared, I wondered what act of fate had saved me. What happened to cause the rifle to misfire? Maybe the water? I watched, praying that she wouldn't return. I tried to ignore the battered knee. Could she have known it was my hockey knee?

The rising moon cast shadows amongst the trees where she had left me, and I noticed something I hadn't realized earlier, something terribly ironic. I was tied to a tree next to the seventh hole at the Crooked Lake Golf Course.

It's where she'd been coming. It's where she had come that day. It's where it had all started, where Ellen, physically capable and mentally deranged had put an end to Harvey's dominion over her.

Leaning back against the tree for support, I felt it give a little. Not in the way a tree bends in the wind, but rather, the way it feels when it's brittle and dead. I leaned against it hard, pushing with all the strength in my good leg. I heard a crack. The trunk began to give way. I pushed harder until it fell. Dried branches rained down on me. With some difficulty I managed to raise my arms behind me until they cleared the ragged trunk. Then I collapsed to the ground where I remained, waiting for my over-taxed leg to stop trembling.

The moon now illuminated the open expanse of the seventh fairway. I was pin-high, twenty-five yards from the hole. A short wedge shot. I leaned against the stump of the dead tree and managed to untie my hands and haul myself into a standing position.

My first step sent excruciating pain shooting through my knee. Determined, I tried another step. And another. With a lopsided, lumbering gate, I continued. The uneven approach to the green and the large sand trap next to it made my progress agonizingly slow.

I could hear the helicopter making another sweep of the lake. I was sure it wouldn't be long before the police found poor Frank's boat piled into the rocks on the south side, where, as Ellen had intended, they would likely concentrate their search.

Having reached the green, I stopped to catch my breath. I again steeled myself against the pain and headed for the park entrance where I hoped to find someone, anyone. My knee had been invaded by pins and needles and had begun to feel mercifully numb.

After what seemed like an eternity, I arrived at the fence and could see, under the streetlight, the kiosk at the gated park entrance. There were no cars in the parking lot and only a dim light showed in the cafeteria. The fence presented another challenge. There was no way I could get over it, so I was forced to lie on the ground and worm my way under. I used the sturdy wooden rails to hoist myself up again. Minutes later I stood leaning on a telephone booth next to the cafeteria where a faint smell of fish and chips lingered. I opened the door to the booth and as I did so the light illuminated an empty cradle where the phone should have been. My hand automatically reached for the handset, but came up with only a medusa of ragged cables. Just as I was about to break the door down to get at the telephone inside the cafeteria, a vehicle rolled down the long hill leading to the park entrance.

Thinking I was now as good as home, I began an awkward hobble over to where it had stopped near the gate. Just as I opened my mouth to shout to the driver, Ellen hurriedly limped out from behind the bushes. At the sight of her, I froze, praying she wouldn't look my way. I watched her approach the vehicle. The door opened and behind the wheel, illuminated by the interior light, sat Harvey's brother, Carl.

Twisting and turning through my mind was the unlikely alliance between Ellen and Carl Kristoff. But then, it made sense. The two who would gain the most by Harvey's death had joined forces. They would circumvent old man Kristoff's divisive will, gain all the current assets that the prenuptial agreement had forestalled and even halt the gifting of two quarters of land worth half a million dollars to the Bender kids. I wondered if this unholy alliance was solely financial.

I stood exposed in the middle of the parking lot, but before I had a chance to move, Carl shifted over and Ellen hauled herself into the driver's seat and closed the door. Idling, the SUV didn't move. The two occupants appeared to be engaged in a heated exchange. I took shelter behind the kiosk. A moment later the Mercedes leaped off the road, hurtling through a barbed wire fence and into a fallow field.

The sound of the motor grew faint. Relief washed over me. Soon I became aware of crickets chattering and mosquitoes buzzing. Before long, two RCMP vehicles with lights flashing and sirens wailing sped down the hill and came to a screeching halt at the gate.

I galloped clumsily toward them. "She's in Harvey's Mercedes," I said to Fred Snell, pointing to the torn barbed wire fence. "And Fred, Harvey's brother is with her." Both vehicles darted through the opening and were soon out of sight. Within minutes the helicopter flew over and another police car raced down the hill and through the opening in the fence. Before long, more lights flashed, but this time it was the ambulance.

"What are you guys doing here?" I asked when they pulled up next to the gate.

"We're here to get you. Got a call from Fred." They rolled out a collapsible gurney and carried it toward me. "He said you could hardly walk."

"Yeah, but I don't need a stretcher," I said, taking a step, and promptly falling flat on my face.

After being strapped on the stretcher and placed in the back of the ambulance, I heard Fred's voice on the radio. "I want you guys up here, just in case." He said that Ellen had taken refuge up on Fogosh Hill behind some Steelco granaries.

In my horizontal position the off-road terrain was a mix of bumps and jumps with the odd thump. We parked behind a police cruiser. The paramedics unstrapped me, and we waited. Floodlights lit up the shiny cylindrical silos.

After a few minutes Fred ducked his way back to where the ambulance was parked. I told him about my little boat ride with Ellen.

"You're telling me the only reason you're not dead is because her gun wouldn't fire?" he said. "Jesus, you're lucky to be alive, aren't you?" He spoke into his shoulder mike, "Sergeant Hutt, apparently her rifle may be inoperative."

"Roger that," Hutt responded and just as he did there was a loud boom. All eyes turned up Fogosh Hill.

"Pull back," Fred said into his mike, "everyone pull back."

"Shotgun," Hutt said.

"Anybody hurt?" Fred asked.

"Negative," Hutt replied.

"Carl must have brought the shotgun," Fred said. "I'll be back at your location in a few minutes, over."

"Where is Carl?" I asked Fred.

"He's in custody. They got stuck in what they thought was a dried out slough. Carl got out and gave up. While we were watching him, Ellen slipped away."

A chill ran through me as I thought of Ellen still on the loose. Fred headed back up the hill while the para-medics took shelter behind their vehicle and lit up. I was left sitting in the passenger seat of the ambulance. As I sat gazing into the darkness I heard a tap on the window. When I turned I saw a shotgun barrel pointed straight at my forehead. And behind it, Ellen Kristoff's terrifying black eyes.

Now she had her chance to finish the job. As if in slow motion, she moved the butt of the shotgun into her shoulder and prepared to fire. Just as it seemed this she-devil would finish me after all, she was distracted by the appearance of the para-medics. Her gun veered in their direction momentarily and as it did I pulled on the door handle, and with all the force I could muster, shoved the heavy door open, ramming it into her. As she toppled over, a blast from the shotgun spit fire straight up into the sky. I dived for her. Her gun was useless at such close range, but as I tried to wrestle it from her, she punched me in the gut. I felt the wind rush out of me and gasped for air. She got to her feet, and pumping another shell into the breech, aimed the gun at me again. But before she could fire, a shot rang out and she fell heavily, landing on top of me. As I struggled to get out from underneath her, I felt the wet warmth of blood pouring out of her motionless body.

21

———————————

The following morning my hospital bed was surrounded by RCMP officers and Crown attorneys who had peppered me with questions, admonished me with looks and even feted me with the odd pat on the back. Fred had told me that Ellen and Carl Kristoff had been charged with the murders of Harvey and Andy. "Ellen's at the University Hospital," he'd said, "they don't know if she'll make it. The bullet passed through her lung and she lost a lot of blood before the paramedics could stop it."

I wanted her to survive. I wanted her tried for the murders she had committed. I wanted Nick to return home, exonerated and I wanted the people of Crooked Lake to again sleep peacefully in their beds.

Doc sent me home with a tensor bandage around my knee and a few pain killers, saying, "We need these beds for sick people." Sitting down to supper that evening, our family joined hands and Rosie gave a prayer of thanks that I had been spared and that peace had been restored to the community. She gave thanks that the Taylors were given a chance to put their lives back together. And typical Rosie, she also asked God to forgive Ellen Kristoff and spare her life, at which Stuart frowned, and finally she prayed that our family be brought under the watchful eye of the Lord.

The Lord must have been listening, because Ellen Kristoff did survive her bullet wound. Defense lawyer Harold Kline argued that Ellen had actually been doing the bidding of Carl Kristoff. When that didn't work, he requested a psychiatric examination, but Judge Kaleniuk had denied this, and Ellen was charged with two counts of first degree murder and numerous other charges, including attempted murder for the poison that was found in my bowl of chili.

Unable to prove that Carl had been directly involved, the police charged him with conspiracy after the fact, aiding and abetting, and a number of other infractions, all of which would keep him from collecting any of Harvey's estate as well as put him behind bars for a long time.

Gerald T. Meyer pled guilty to aggravated assault and coupled with his bar room antics netted two years less a day, which he was happy to take, so relieved was he that he hadn't killed his brother. He swore to the judge that he would, henceforth, follow the straight and narrow. He also agreed to undergo treatment for alcoholism.

The completed development application had been found in Harvey's papers and the two quarters of land would soon be in the hand's of Stella Bender's two kids. The judge had even made allowance for Frank Baumgartner's wrecked boat.

Leaving the courthouse the day of sentencing, I caught sight of Juliette Riskowsky who'd been called as a prosecution witness. She waved at me from across the expansive foyer, which prompted Rosie to pinch my upper arm, hard. Wincing, I waved, but Juliette didn't see me, as she'd already turned and was walking away, her arm through that of a young man with broad shoulders and blond hair. It might have been Josh, but I doubted it.

"Well, Bartholomew," Nick said as he teed up his ball on the seventh hole, "you did one hell of a job. And I should add, I expected nothing less from an old-timer like you." He lined up for the shot, waggled, then stepped away from his ball. "You know, maybe you should get out of the fishing business and become a private dick." A grin peeked out from under his bushy moustache.

"Are you gonna hit the ball?" Doc Chow said, anxious to improve his score.

"Yeah, this hole gives me the heebie-jeebies," said Dee Elliot who'd recently taken up golf, and was doing surprisingly well with the aid of a little plastic booklet that she referred to before each shot.

Nick's expert shot landed within a few feet of the cup and as it continued to roll, everyone howled for a hole in one. The ball came up just inches short.

He shoved his new seven iron back into his bag, cracked a can of *Pil* and grinned from ear to ear. "Okay Doc," he said, "let's see you top that."

That evening Randall carried a tray loaded with hamburger patties out to the deck where I'd been heating up the barbeque. I was glad to see him back, despite Annie's condition, or maybe because of it. Annie followed him out with plates, paper napkins and condiments.

"Did you guys pack your long underwear?" I said.

"Oh Daddy, it's not that bad," she wrapped her arms around Randall's middle, "and besides, on cold nights we can keep each other warm."

I looked off into the field toward the United Church Cemetery where I knew Mom and Dad would be sending blessings to these two young people who were going to bring another life, my grandchild, into the world.

"So, Daddy, did you know that Randy's benefits include two trips a year to the destination of our choice anywhere in Canada." While getting some space down in Moose Jaw, Randall had managed to get a job with an environmental company; in Nunavut Territory, of all places. Thankfully, he would still be able to do the Stuart Lake environmental study before he and Annie left for Iqaluit in the fall. Annie said, "Let's see, maybe we'll go someplace romantic, like Montreal or maybe Vancouver."

"You'll be coming right back here, young lady," Rosie said, carrying out a basket of hamburger buns. "That baby's going to want to see her grandmother."

"Or *his* grandfather," I said.

"And I'm sure Randall's parents will be just as anxious as we are," Rosie said.

"Where's the wedding gonna be?" Stuart asked, already spreading gobs of mayonnaise and mustard on a bun.

"St. Andrews Church," Annie said. This brought a frown to Rosie's face, who would have preferred the wedding take place at Crooked Lake United. "It's on the university campus," Annie added, then turned to her younger brother and said, "We'd like you to be an usher, Stu."

Stuart put down his hamburger bun and blushed a little. "Okay. What do I have to do?"

"It's a very important job," I put in. "You have to keep the families on separate sides of the church, so no fights break out during the ceremony."

Rosie frowned at me. "We'll have to get you a new suit, Stu."

"And what about my dress," Annie said, "will it be ready for a fitting before we leave?"

"Yes," Rosie said, "but of course it will need alterations right up until the wedding day."

Later, when the house was quiet, Rosie and I lay in bed holding hands. "So what did Sergeant Hutt have to say?" Rosie asked.

"He said they might never have caught Ellen had I not been such a snoop."

"Almost a compliment," Rosie said.

We lay in comfortable silence for a time.

"I'm glad it's all over," Rosie said.

I took a deep, satisfying breath. "Yeah, me too." We heard some water running, a door close, then more silence.

"So what did the letter say?" Rosie asked, referring to the envelope that still lay unopened on my desk. It was from Saskatchewan Environment and Resource Management.

"As usual," I said, "a lot of bureaucratic mumbo-jumbo." I felt her body tense, so I made up some mumbo-jumbo. "They're trying to balance tourism with resource exploitation and said that environmental impact studies will play a big part in their determinations."

"Well that sounds positive, and if Randall's study can help…"

"Yup." But I didn't want to go into it at the moment, because Rosie had rolled over and put a hand on my belly. She laid her smooth leg across mine and tickled my neck with her tongue.

"Tired?" she breathed.

"No."

"Good." And her hand began to slide. "How's your knee?"

"Just a little stiff."

She giggled. "Bart, promise me something…"

"What's that?"

"That you won't get involved in anything like this again."

"I promise," I said, kissing her on the mouth. 'Course, at that moment, I would have promised her just about anything, eh.

To purchase a copy of *Crooked Lake*,
or to pre-purchase your signed copy of
Nelson Brunanski's next small-town mystery, *Frost Bite*
please contact:

Caronel Publishing Inc.

Vancouver Canada

Telephone 604 253-2229

caronel@uniserve.com

www.caronelpublishing.com

————————————

A short excerpt from
Frost Bite

where Bart Bartowski sticks his nose in, again...

Car lights played across the window.

"He's here," Rosie said. "Did Stuart tell you about his hockey thing?"

"His hockey thing?"

"His thing. . .his support, she waved at herself obliquely. "I don't know what you call it. But I do know what it's for, so you spend what ever it takes to get the best."

"Yes, mam," I saluted.

The storm door protested loudly as I broke the frosty barrier that had built up over night. I crossed the crisp snow to Tom's Dodge Ram, my boots squeaking in the thirty-below prairie morning.

In praise of *Crooked Lake*

"I loved your book, I couldn't put it down." *PP*

Crooked Lake: a funny novel with a very likable hero.
Saskatoon StarPhoenix

"It's a great whodunit—it fooled me."
Paul Grescoe, Winner of the Canadian Crime Writers' Award

"It was a hoot. I laughed all the way through it." *TL*

Crooked Lake is bound to catch on. *CBC*

"A Saturday night romp down a winding country road."
Stephen Scriver winner of the W.O Mitchell Award

"Move over Corner Gas." *PR*

"I really liked your book. So did my husband, *and* my
daughter." *CS*

Times-Herald names Brunanski winner of mystery writing
contest. (July '05)
Moose-Jaw Times-Herald

"Like calamine lotion on an insect bite, this work of
fiction is a balm to the spirit." *MS*

"When's the next one coming out?"